WRONG DEVIL

DARK REIGN

MIKA LANE

HEADLANDS PUBLISHING

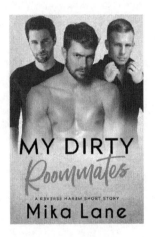

The last thing I expect when I take a job in a new town is to end up living with three smoking hot roommates. Who also happen to be personal trainers. They are so out of my league, and I am so out of my element. But I can't afford to live alone in San Francisco, so have resigned myself to sharing.

Apparently, these guys like to share too…
Overhearing them say I'm cute gives me a nice ego boost. But I want to get in shape, and they'll only help me under one condition…
I have to do *whatever* they tell me to, *whenever* they tell me to do it. Instead of scaring me, the thought of being at their
beck and call sounds hot. And once they start with their naughty demands, I want them to never stop.
They work me hard in the gym and everywhere else.

This whole roommate situation just put a new spin on 'sharing.'

COPYRIGHT

manner whatsoever without the express written permission of the publisher except for the use of quotations in a book review.

Like deals and other cool stuff?
Sign up for my newsletter!

RUSSIAN ENDEARMENTS

babushka: grandmother
krastotka: gorgeous
malishka: baby girl
zolotse: darling

CHAPTER ONE

ABBY

"YOU CAN'T WEAR *THAT*."

I knew I'd made a mistake hanging out with these girls.

Sabine bends to rub a little more self-tanner on her already-tan calves, and as she does, her micro-mini dress, the one she dug out of the corner of her suitcase for tonight's 'clubbing,' hitches up, exposing a full view of her ass and the thong panty doing little to cover her privates.

I guess that's kind of the point.

Christ. Wait till they see my white cotton granny panties.

I'd been sitting in a tapas restaurant, one of

about a gazillion in Madrid, when these two sisters happened by my table.

"Oh, hello!" the taller one calls, jumping and waving with enough gusto to attract the attention of the whole restaurant.

I wave back, of course, because I'm polite that way, although I'm not sure why they're acting like they just spotted a long-lost friend or some such.

Encouraged by my wave, they weave their way between the extremely tight tables, turning heads and bumping diners with their hips and oversized purses, even causing one man to drop a piece of the octopus he's eating right into his lap.

The girls make no notice.

Breathless, they reach my table. There's one empty chair, so they plop down, sharing it. Two asses on a tiny bistro chair.

Ouch.

One of them reaches for my water and takes a sip. Really.

I pull my small dish of *patatas bravas* closer and hold my fork tighter.

"We know you!" the smaller one exclaims in heavily accented English. "We're staying in the same Airbnb. We saw you at, um, how do you say? *Petit dejeuner?*" She looks at the other girl.

"*Breakfast*," the other one says, rolling her eyes. She turns back to me. "We saw you at *breakfast*."

I nod politely. "I… I saw you too," I say, trying to match their enthusiasm.

"I'm Sabine," says the short one, "and this is my sister Vivianne. Or, you can call us Sabi and Vivi." She extends a hand.

"*Sabeen* and *Veeveeawn*," I repeat to make sure I get them right, even though the nicknames are way easier. "You're French?"

Sabine nods and shimmies her shoulders when I return her handshake.

"We know Americans like to shake hands rather than *faire la bise*. You know, kiss cheeks." She looks at her sister, who nods in approval.

"I'm Abby," I say, popping the last *patatas brava* on my plate into my mouth.

"Abby," Vivianne repeats like *Abbay*. I like it, though. It sounds exotic. "Why are you alone?" she asks, scrunching up her face.

Wow. This one doesn't beat around the bush.

Why am I alone?

I'm pretty much always alone. Hell, I spend so much time alone I don't even know what it's like to hang out with someone.

Unless that someone is my dad. I'm with him a lot. In short, he's needy. And possessive.

But it doesn't matter, this business of being alone. I don't mind it. I'm not a cool girl. Not by any stretch of the imagination. I have spent the majority of my life with my nose in a book, naturally under the close watch of Dad. Some might say *obsessive* watch. But that's understandable. I'm the only family he has since my mom bailed.

That I'm more than four thousand miles from home at this moment is a miracle in itself. I pretty much extorted Dad to let me take this trip, threatening not to return to college in the fall for my junior year. Would I really have done that? Probably not. But he finally relented, as long as I promised to follow a strict itinerary and call home every day.

Plus, my twenty-first birthday is soon, and I wanted to be someplace exciting to celebrate it. After a lot of persuading, I convinced him to give me this as a gift. He was opposed at first, but to my surprise, I eventually wore him down.

He gave me a decent budget to work with. Not enough to get into trouble, but enough to keep a roof over my head and keep from starving while on the road. I've never been out of the USA, so Spain seemed like a manageable place to start. Good food, cool history, safe for a girl on her own. At least that's what all the travel sites say.

"I... I do a lot alone," I say in response to their nosy-ass question.

Confusion crosses Sabi's face, like something's been lost in translation. But a second later she follows up with another bright smile.

"*Abbay*, would you like to hang out—that's what Americans say, right? *hang out?*—with us?"

They look so hopeful. And hell, there isn't anything else on my day's agenda besides visiting the Prado museum and walking around. They seem nice enough. And fun.

But they also look like they're from the 'cool girls' table.' And cool girls don't hang out with the likes of me.

Regardless of my flash-back lunchroom status, Vivi puts her hands on the table. "We would also like to practice our English," she adds.

And there we have it. Although their English sounds pretty good to me.

"I'm going for a semester in America, and I need practice." She looks at her sister, who nods enthusiastically.

I shrug, glad I washed my hair this morning. Regardless, I probably look like these girls' poor cousin, anyway. "Yeah. Okay. Let's do it," I say, trying to muster enthusiasm.

I trudge after Sabi and Vivi as we wander

9

around Madrid, me in my faded denim skirt and high-top Converse Chucks, kind of like the less-pretty friend who holds the alpha girl's hair back when she barfs. The sisters turn heads and giggle at catcalls everywhere they go in their short summer dresses and platform shoes, flipping their hair like preening peacocks, and it's all just fascinating to observe.

As usual, I am invisible. But I'm used to that.

We exit the Prado museum after a rushed visit —no surprise, these girls couldn't care less about art—and even though I'm in my most comfy shoes, my feet are aching. I have no idea how these two clomp around all day in platform shoes. When they see the pain on my face, we plop down on a bench vacated by some noisy Americans and Vivianne coaxes me into a selfie with her sister. She shows us all the photo, and then jumps to her feet.

"*Abbay*, you must come with us tonight!" she screams.

Sabi grabs my arm. "Oh, yes, *Abbay*. You must."

I figure they're going to dinner someplace nice. Which is fine. I'm not getting close to spending my daily budget, saving some each day so I can splurge when the impulse hits me.

Or they have plans for a show. I've been

thinking about seeing a Flamenco exhibition. It's a must-see according to all the guidebooks.

"What's tonight?" I ask, wondering if I'll be sorry I didn't just say I have plans.

Vivi claps her hands together. "We're going to Ibiza! We have an Airbnb, and we have passes to the *hottest* club there."

What the fuck is *eebeetha*?

It doesn't really matter. They lost me at *club*.

"Yeah, thanks. But I don't think so. I told my dad I'd stick to the schedule here in Spain."

"But it's *in* Spain, *Abbay*! It's a beautiful little island in the Mediterranean, only an hour plane ride away," Sabi says. "Oh, you're coming with us. I'm buying you a ticket right now." She whips out her phone and says something in French to her sister.

Now it's my turn to jump to my feet. "No, Sabine, don't. Don't buy me a ticket. I can't go."

I don't care if Ibiza *is* part of Spain and only one hour away, if my father finds out, he'll drag my ass home. Besides, I don't do clubs. Not my thing. Not my style.

She ignores me. Of course. "Oh my god, these flights are so cheap. Okay, *Abbay*, give me your passport number," she says, looking expectantly at me, finger poised and ready on the airline app.

But before I can protest one final time, Vivi grabs my hand, twirling me like we're dancing. Then she twirls herself.

This is how pretty girls act. Like life is a buffet table, waiting for them to decide what they want to try next.

Me, not so much. I mean, it's not like I'm not curious. It's not like I don't want to experience things. I made it all the way to Spain from Miami, for cripe's sake. But I'm just not used to... going for it, mainly because... Dad. Yeah, he keeps me on a short leash. But I am working on changing that...

He needs to get a life. There. I said it.

Sabi shows me her phone screen. "All I need, *Abbay*, is your passport number and I can buy your ticket. Come on. Say you'll come. Ibiza is beautiful and we'll dance all night long."

I've never danced all night long. I've never done anything all night long. Except sleep.

Vivi puts her hands on either side of my face. "Come on, Abby. Join us. It will be so much fun."

She's so pretty and so hopeful and for a moment I want to be just like her, so I get sucked right in, like Alice in Wonderland falling down the rabbit hole.

I pull my passport out of my bag.

DEAR GOD, what have I done?

I lug my suitcase up the stairs of the Ibiza Airbnb Vivi and Sabi booked, sweat dripping down my temples and between my boobs. The owner or landlord or whatever he is, took the girls' suitcases, one in each hand, which left me to handle my own.

Because, of course.

After I caved and gave Sabi my passport number outside of the Prado museum, she booked my ticket, and the two sisters jumped up and down and screamed. When they realized I was standing there looking at them, partially in shock and completely petrified Dad would cut me off if he found out, they took my hands and made a *ring around the rosy* circle.

I can't lie. Their exuberance and lightness—I can't think of anything else to call it—are infectious. In the face of my life as a responsible, if repressed, daughter, I couldn't help but start to laugh and jump up and down with them.

I'm going to Ibiza! To a club! And I don't even know what Ibiza is!

My new life starts today.

But the cab ride from Ibiza's airport to the

Airbnb tells me just about all I need to know. We pass fancy resorts, villas built into the hillsides, and lots and lots of good-looking people like Sabi and Vivi out walking, talking, laughing, and just generally having fun.

I can totally see why they wanted to come here.

And I can totally see why I should not have. But hell, I'm here, they paid for my flight and the Airbnb, so I'm not giving up yet.

I'm starting a new life. Right?

The girls plop onto our room's beds after the manager hands a key over and leaves us.

"Oh my god, it's so beautiful here!" Sabi laughs.

Vivi falls back on the bed and kicks her legs in the air, I can only guess as a way to show her excitement.

She bolts upright and inhales deeply. "Mmmm. Smell that ocean air. Madrid's *nothing* like this."

Fair enough. Madrid's not near the ocean. But it's still nice. If you ask me.

Sabi checks the time on her phone. "Get dressed, girls, the night is waiting!"

In moments, the girls are in their club gear— the aforementioned micro-minis, high heels, and enough makeup to fill a drugstore.

I pull out my 'edgiest' outfit—a pair of hole-y

jeans and a black T-shirt. I can instantly tell that the French sisters do not approve.

"Hmmm," Sabi says while her sister takes the self-tanner from her. "Is that all you have?"

I look down. Yeah, it's all I fucking have if you're talking about wearing dresses that let your cooch hang out.

"Mmm-hmm."

She digs into her own bag and pulls out something that looks like a handkerchief. Or a rag. And tosses it my way.

"Wear this top. It's better than what you have on."

I dutifully pull my T-shirt off and replace it with a skimpy little tank top that barely covers my breasts.

She rolls her eyes. "The bra. Take the bra off."

I look down. If I take off my bra, I will be quite... exposed. I mean, covered-up enough for a club, but not enough to go anywhere else.

Which, I guess, is fine. If these girls have their coochies almost hanging out, I guess I can have my tits almost hanging out.

"Okay, girls," Vivianne says, looking in the mirror one last time.

I stuff my money, ID, and passport in the back

pocket of my jeans, and swipe on some red lipstick. The only lipstick I own.

"Abby, did you put your passport in the safe?" Sabine asks.

I feel my back pocket, where my passport is safe and sound. If there's one thing my father drilled into my head before I left Miami, it was to never, ever be without my passport. He might be a pain in my ass, but this advice sounded solid.

"No, I'm good," I say, heading for the door.

Let's get the party started before I change my mind and spend the night at the Airbnb reading a book on my phone, waiting for the girls to return.

But Vivi grabs my arm. "No! You cannot bring your passport to the club. It will get lost for sure." Her eyes are wide with fear.

I look at her tight grip on my arm, and then at Sabi, who nods, and points to the safe.

"I… I think I'll keep mine on me. I'll just be really careful."

The sisters look at each other and simultaneously shake their heads. "No," Sabi says, holding out her hand. "We cannot let you do that. It would be crazy."

"And stupid," Vivi adds. "It will be crowded and anyone could steal it from you. You brush up against someone on the dance floor and *poof!* it's gone."

Well, shit. I've already defied Dad by getting on a plane and leaving Madrid, so what's one more broken rule?

"Fine," I say.

I walk over to Sabine and look inside the safe, which holds their French passports and her laptop. I toss mine inside, and she slams the door shut.

"What's the code? You know, to get it back open?" I ask.

"Easy," Vivi answers. "One-two-three-four."

Really? Like that's not the first thing any thief would try. But whatever.

After about fifteen minutes of the club, my head is pounding from the throbbing house music, the pot smoke in the air, and the smell of hot bodies grinding against each other in the unair-conditioned space.

But hey, I'm living my best life.

I leave the dance floor and push my way up to the bar, ready to order a beer, which I can do since the drinking age in Spain is only eighteen. But before I can, Vivi appears with her sister in tow, smiling broadly, sweaty from dancing.

"Oh my god, don't buy a drink," she says, shouting over the house music. "Here. Look what someone gave us." Three tiny pills sit in the palm of her hand.

Oh, for Christ's sake.

I don't know shit about drugs. Except not to take them.

"What is it?" I ask.

The sisters look at each other and roll their eyes. "*Abbay*, do you never get out? Doesn't everyone in America party and take drugs? These are ecstasy."

Yeah, pretty sure I don't want any of that.

Vivianne pulls a water bottle out of her purse, and she and her sister each down a pill.

"Here," she says, raising her palm to my face like I might eat the pill out of her hand.

I back up, bumping into the people behind me. They don't notice. "No thanks. I don't want it."

She shrugs, pops it into her mouth, and chugs some more water.

Vivianne shrieks with laughter and claps her sister on the back. "Crazy," she yells. "My sister is crazy." She grabs her hand and leads her back to the dance floor.

"Ibiza is a wild place. It's always smart to be careful," a male voice says close to my ear.

Very close to my ear.

I whip around to see a guy about my height,

with glasses, wearing a faded concert T-shirt and low-slung jeans held up by a wide belt.

I don't expect anyone to chat me up, especially in a place full of women who look like supermodels.

But I could hang. This guy's the only male who's spoken to me this entire trip, aside from waiters and shopkeepers.

"Oh, you know," I say breezily, like I am offered ecstasy all the time, "I'm just not in the mood."

His eyebrows rise like he can see right through my crap. "Good thinking. Can I get you a beer?" He waves at the bartender, who pretty much comes running.

"Yeah, sure," I say, watching them fist bump.

"So, where are you from?" he asks.

Holy crap. Am I actually meeting someone on vacation?

I watch the bartender open my beer bottle and don't take my eyes off it until it's in my hand. Another thing the guidebooks say. It's ice cold and feels so good going down. "Miami. You?" I ask, looking around the club like I'm all cool and stuff.

"Chicago. But I'm on tour this summer."

I spot the sisters on the edge of the dance floor chatting with some guys. I wave casually. They don't see me.

"On tour?" I ask, trying to sound bored.

He smiles at me. He seems pretty normal. "I'm a DJ and am doing a tour this summer." He points to a stand above the dance floor holding a bunch of speakers and other equipment.

"Who's playing the music right now?" I ask, wondering if he's bullshitting me.

I wouldn't be surprised.

He raises a finger and taps his temple. Yeah, I know I'm not a dumbshit, dude.

"It's a tape right now. But I gotta get back up there. Want to see it?"

I look back at the platform and it's wide open —no doors or glass or anything. Looks safe enough.

How many times in my life will I be invited to hang with a DJ in a popular Ibiza nightclub?

"Yeah. Okay," I say.

I look around for the French sisters who, for some reason, I feel responsible for. That's me. Always the responsible one. But if they're going to get wasted or whatever on ecstasy, someone has to keep an eye out for them.

"Let me just tell me friends where I'm going," I say, gesturing toward them.

"Oh my god," Sabi says, throwing an arm around my neck when she spots me. "This is our

American friend," she says to the guys she's talking to.

"Isn't this fun?" Vivi screams, grabbing my hand.

The guys turn and nod at the DJ, who's now standing next to me.

"So. Much. Fun," Vivi screams again, now yanking on my arm. "Let's go!"

Let's go where?

To my surprise, the DJ pries her fingers from me, separating us. "Sorry, honey. She's coming with me."

Okay, now people are fighting over me?

"Come on, Abby. Let me show you the DJ booth," he says, throwing an arm around my shoulder and pulling me. Hard

The sisters' eyes widen at his forcefulness, and they glance at the guys they're talking to.

"Hold on," I say, trying to pull away.

But I can't.

And how did this guy know my name? We never exchanged names.

"Let her go!" Vivi says, pulling me again, this time to wrest me from the DJ.

While she does this, one of the guys steps up and gets in the DJ's face. "Hey. Looks like she wants you to let her go."

A strange look passes over the DJ's face, so different from his expression of just a few minutes before when he bought me my beer.

What the hell's going on?

He juts out his chin and steps closer to the guy confronting him. But the DJ is no match for him at several inches shorter and about half as wide.

"Fuck you," he spits, and takes off, disappearing into the crowd.

Well. Dodged a bullet there. And so much for my vacation romance.

"Oh my god," Sabi says with a hand to her chest. "Thank you so much. You saved my friend."

She takes my other arm and runs her hand up and down it like she's stroking a cat. "*Abbay*, these handsome gentlemen invited us to their boat. It's docked in the marina just down the street."

I lean close to Sabine's ear. "We don't know them."

Although being on a boat in Ibiza does sound fucking cool.

She apparently doesn't notice my whisper. "Oh, *Abbay*. They are super nice. I can tell. And they just saved you from that terrible man!"

The guys look at me, smiling, now that they know I am opposed to going on their boat.

One of them, the taller, extends a hand my way,

and damn if his chin dimple doesn't make my heart skip a beat. "Hello, Abby. I'm Ilya."

Ilya? What kind of name is that?

He continued. "And this is Fedor."

Fedor? Russian?

He bows his head. "Very nice to meet you, Abby. Please join us. It's a beautiful night."

Well, shit. Even in the dim of the club, his light-blue eyes, rimmed by thick black eyelashes, are so freaking... sexy. And he's looking at me. Like really looking at me.

Guys like that don't look at girls like me. It's not that there's anything wrong with me, it's just that prettiness is currency. A currency I don't have.

Regardless, they are inviting us on their boat.

"You guys," I repeat to the sisters, "we don't know them."

But there's no resolve behind my protest. I know I'm just blowing hot air. Everyone else knows I'm just blowing hot air.

They move closer, ganging up on me. "*Abbay*," Sabi says, stroking my hair, "they are much cuter than the DJ. Who doesn't even have a boat."

She and Vivi dissolve into giggles.

Guess this is what ecstasy does.

Sabi puts her hands together like she's praying and begs. "Please, *Abbay*. We will not go without

23

you. We need you because you are not wasted like we are."

They start giggling again.

"*Abbay*, please? They look so nice," she pleads.

Fedor, the one with the eyes, approaches our little confab. "Don't worry, ladies. We understand. You don't know us. You should stay here and enjoy your evening."

He waves, and with his friend, heads toward the door.

I watch the crowd part for them, both women and men admiring them—their handsome faces, T-shirts straining around their biceps, jeans hugging their perfect asses.

Oh shit, oh shit, oh shit.

"Wait!" I call after them.

Why the fuck shouldn't I have my fun?

I've been letting my father dictate my every move since... well, since Mom left. But I'm freaking twenty years old with two years of college under my belt. I'm a long way from home, and I sure as hell have never been invited on a boat, in Ibiza, with two of the most handsome guys I've ever seen. And, my birthday is coming up.

I've already left Madrid, gone out without my passport, talked with a creepy, possessive DJ guy, and sent the last three phone calls from my father directly to voicemail.

So, I might as well go full-on bad girl, and see what other trouble I can get myself into.

"Wait, wait," I call, chasing after them with the sisters behind me, giggling their asses off. "We'll go. We'll go to your boat."

CHAPTER TWO

BOGDAN

I FUCKING hate Ibiza party girls.

To an extent, anyway.

But it's inevitable that Ilya and Fedor drag a couple back to the boat, as they often do.

Not that I don't benefit from my associates' charm. Girls on vacation don't come to Ibiza because they're nuns. The want to party. They want to get laid. And I am here for it all. Give them a story to take back to their friends stuck at home. Give them a memory of one of their 'wildest' trips ever, when some good-looking guys invited them out on a boat and fucked the stuffing out of them. Sometimes they have their first threesome or foursome with us. Sometimes, they mess around with their girlfriends too. Kiss, eat some pussy, or maybe even ass if we guys are feeling really persuasive. It's all on the menu.

Remember that time? I can hear them saying some few years down the road. *What was that guy's name again, the one I met in Ibiza?*

Which is fine because I never remember their names, either. That is, if I bother to ask to begin with. Which I normally don't.

I toss aside the book I'm reading, take one last draw on my scotch, and stretch, looking up at the black night and the glittering stars. It's a freakishly still night, so the boat's rocking is at a minimum.

I'll say this much about Ibiza. We're far enough from Spain's mainland that there's minimal light pollution, which makes for amazing night skies. Not that the majority of people who come here ever even notice.

The big locked gate at the end of the dock clangs open and then closes again. Laughter draws nearer as do footsteps, and it's clear several people are on their way down to our slip. The guys must have had a successful night. They usually do.

I extend a hand to help this evening's company aboard, two dolled-up babes who sound French, and their quieter friend, who might be unnoticeable in the dim light if she wasn't wearing bright red lipstick.

She's a novelty, not trying too hard. Actually, she's not trying at all. Which is kind of hot. Like a challenge

"Welcome aboard, ladies," I say with a slight bow. "Please remove your shoes while Karol gets a couple bottles of champagne. I am Bogdan, but you can call me Bogi if you like."

Fed turns on the music, and with champagne in their hands minutes later, the French girls begin to dance.

It's not like I have anything against party girls, aside from the fact that they can be a pain in the ass. The pretty ones are the worst. They're accustomed to the universe giving them what they want, and when they don't get it, watch out. I can't blame a person for being demanding, but some of the chicks the guys bring back to the yacht are downright ridiculous.

A while back, a woman dancing up on the bow dropped an earring or something into the water. She actually wanted us guys to dive in and find it for her.

Tonight's girls aren't so bad, at least not so far. The two who identified themselves as sisters are definitely on something, cooing and bumping and grinding against each other. Probably took some of that shit ecstasy they give out in the clubs. Why anyone would take street drugs from people they don't know is beyond me. I mean, moving drugs is one of our best businesses, but I never take the shit.

I want to live to see my thirty-fourth birthday.

But hey, when people are on vacation, they do stuff they don't do at home. Myself, I pretty much do whatever the fuck I want whether I'm home or not.

My line of business affords that luxury.

Their friend with the red lips, however, clearly did not indulge. She's clear eyed, sitting in a far corner of the afterdeck, holding her champagne like it's poison.

I chat her up. Find out how the hell she ended up hanging with girls like these.

"You do not like champagne. What a terrible host I am," I say, taking her glass from her. "Can I get you something else to drink... what did you say your name was?"

She gets to her feet, swaying slightly, unaccustomed to the slight movement of the boat. "Abby. My name is Abby. And if you don't mind, I would like something else to drink, thank you."

"Karol!" I shout.

Our steward and all-round-everything man pokes his head up from the galley. "Yes, Bogi," he says in his heavy Polish accent.

"Can you take my friend here, Abby, down and show her our selection of beverages? Let her choose something other than champagne."

Karol gives his usual small smile, designed to hide his bad teeth.

I know this about him. He's been with my family since I was a little kid.

"Miss Abby, come, come," he says, waving her toward him.

Abby looks at me. "Cool. Thanks."

By letting her choose her own drink, Abby can be confident no drugs were added to it. Unlike her French friends, with their imbibing of street drugs, Abby is the kind of girl that only drinks things she's seen opened.

Smart move.

Too many girls accept drinks from total strangers, and the results, sadly, are often ugly. I might not be the nicest guy in the world, but I don't fucking drug women.

I'll kill a guy who does shit like that.

In fact, I just about have. The guys and I saw some guy trying to roofie a girl in a club a while back. We beat the shit out of him until an ambulance was called.

No regrets there.

Not that I ever regret things, anyway.

I know what was behind that fury then, not that it's left me. It lives barely beneath the surface of who I am, bubbling to the top every now and then, whether I like it or not. Rage around losing your little sister to uncaring fucks will do that to you. Especially when it's your own damn fault.

Abby comes back with a beer and a grateful smile on her face. "Thank you, Bogi."

"You are a smart one, Abby," I say, leading her to a seat. "You have to be careful. Unlike your friends here. Tell me, how it is you are vacationing with them?"

She looks at them and shrugs. "I'm not really vacationing with them. We were staying at the same Airbnb in Madrid. They invited me to come to Ibiza for the night."

I study her and see, now that I'm closer, she's actually pretty. Very pretty. And with a couple tweaks, she could be even more appealing. But I'm sensing that's not important to her. She doesn't glide by on her looks. She could, although I doubt she knows that. She doesn't seem the type to trade on things like that.

"Do you like to read, Abby?" I ask, leaning back to watch a shooting star.

Even in the dim light I can see her eyes widen with the hope that she's found someone she has something in common with. All night she's probably felt like a fish out of water, and it's a relief for her to talk about something she likes.

"I love to read," she says. "What about you?"

I nod, glad I'm close enough to see little curls springing up around her hairline, thanks to the damp sea air. What would she look like if she released that bun at the back of her neck?

On the other hand, I like that her hair is pulled up. It allows me to see her neck. And fuck if it isn't one I'd like to have a little nibble on. Just until she winces from the pain.

But first things first.

"I am a reader, Abby. Always have been. You see, I didn't have a chance to go to college. So, I educate myself. It's a lifelong process."

She studies me, most likely wanting to ask how it is the guys and I own a yacht that happens to be docked in Ibiza.

But she's too polite to ask. She's well brought up.

Across the afterdeck, everyone is dancing to Earth, Wind, and Fire, and I can't deny my foot's tapping to what Fedor always calls 'the ultimate fuckin' dance music.' If I want to show Abby a good time, and thus have a good time myself, I need to get her moving a little.

I stand before her, extending a hand. She looks at me, then the others dancing, swigs the last of her beer, and gets up.

That the French girls are a foregone conclusion, a dalliance so certain it doesn't even deserve to be called a conquest, having paired off with Fed and Ilya, is no surprise. The guys will soon have them in their rooms and the night air will be filled with the moans and groans of vacation sex. Karol already has the captain taking us out to the open water, where our noise won't get us kicked out the marina, which has a strict no partying after midnight rule.

Seems kind of silly for Ibiza, but whatever.

As we get a bit further from shore, Ilya turns up the sound and we dance hard, harder than minutes before. So hard I don't think the girls even realize we are no longer docked.

Even Abby seems to have shed her air of caution, the sisters' enthusiasm, drug-fueled or not, having rubbed off on her. She's let her hair down, both figuratively and literally. A wild mane of curls surrounds her head, expanding as she

34

twirls and jumps, laughs and shakes her head. Her little top occasionally slips, baring a small breast or two, and her bright red lipstick and smile are nothing but delicious.

And I'd like to put them to good use.

Now that's she's happy and having a good time, she's downright beautiful.

I can't take my eyes off her. She has no idea. But she will.

Fed and Ilya place their hands on the French girls' hips, obviously grinding against their asses. The sisters respond by reaching behind themselves to grind right back. Their short dresses have ridden up, past the V between their legs, displaying a lacy thong on one and a sheer one on the other, barely covering their shaved pussies. They desperately want a taste, or maybe more than a taste, of all that Fed and Ilya have to offer.

It won't surprise me if they pull down their panties and bend over right here, on the boat's afterdeck. It wouldn't be the first time.

It would make the crew, who are probably all awake by now and spying on us from the upper level, quite happy.

Rather than responding to the sisters' display, Abby simply laughs at the girls' hedonism, like this is normal. Like she sees this every day.

Like she wants it for herself.

Maybe she does.

I turn her to face me, placing my hands on either side of her face, and press my lips to hers. It's a risky effort, making such a bold move on a girl who's spent more of her life watching the party rather than joining in, but she moves her lips against mine in response, slowly parting them so I can taste her, explore her soft mouth, and give her an inkling of other things I have in store for her. She surprises me in how she gets lost in our kiss, gradually pressing herself to me, arms around my neck. I continue to lightly rock in time to the music, and she follows, like I'm leading her in the kind of slow dance teenagers do when they're trying to be romantic but also cop a feel without anyone around them noticing.

By the time we part and come up for air, we find ourselves alone on the deck. Sometime during our kiss, the other four disappeared, no doubt to get started fucking before dawn breaks and the magic of the evening, not to mention the ecstasy, wears off. The morning after nights like this are rough, like a pretty glass falling and breaking into pointy shards. The girls' makeup will be smeared, their hair a mess, their eyes half closed from lack of sleep, and their skin will be sallow and splotchy from crappy street drugs. They will complete their walk of shame, staggering back to their accommodations and sleep most of the day away like many of the partiers on the island.

If I've seen it once, I've seen it a hundred times.

"Let's go," I say to Abby, and take her by the hand.

She follows me with no resistance, probably having resigned herself to getting 'the whole vacation experience.' Once in my cabin, I remove her jeans and top. I lay her on the edge of my bed, her ass all but hanging off, and get to my knees. The scent of her musky excitement has me vibrating, and even if she begged me to stop now, I wouldn't.

But I'll let her think she has a choice.

"You good, baby?" I whisper.

She's silent for a moment and I wonder if she's going to raise an objection. It would be such an inconvenience.

"Yeah," she says. "Vacation sex. Another box to tick off."

I have to laugh at how she's surrendering to a checklist, practical to the end, even when she is about to get her pussy eaten. But I can fuck that out of her, if not tonight, then another. We'll have plenty of time.

Not that she knows that.

I slash my tongue through her lips, tasting the cream from her opening, stopping only at her clit, the hard little bud begging for attention. I create a suction that has her bucking her hips into my face, silently pleading for more.

She lies back, her hair sprawling, hands on tits, tossing her head as I swirl her clit between my lips.

I pull back as her breathing gets raspy. Her eyes fly open, and she looks up at me in alarm.

Or is it frustration?

I enjoy both.

"Open your mouth," I say. I take two fingers and put them in her mouth as far as she can take them. "Suck, Abby. Make them wet so I can fuck you with them."

Her eyes fall closed, and she licks and slurps until my fingers are wet. I place them at the entrance to her cunt, slowly wriggling my way inside her. She's so hot and so tight, just like I knew she'd be, and when I've worked my way inside her, I start a 'come here' motion with my fingers that brings her to her edge.

Her hips push into my hand for more, so I begin to pump. She writhes and tosses her head, her breath punctuated by sighs, moans, and little laughs.

With my free hand, I adjust my dick in my

pants. The only way I'll be getting off tonight is by myself, which is fine. My priority is to make this girl feel good. To make her feel as beautiful as she is.

I will make her believe this if it's the last thing I do.

"Oh, oh, oh," she moans, and she contracts around my fingers. I want to put more inside her, maybe even fist her, but that will wait for another time. We'll work up to that.

And with a gasp, she convulses, thrashing lightly on the bed, alternately clenching her fingers, opening them, and clenching again. As she comes down, I withdraw my hand, now covered in her delicious juices and move her up on the bed. I pull back the comforter and tuck her under it. With a kiss on the forehead, I turn off the light and leave her.

Back on deck, I find Karol returning from shore with the tender. He switches off the small boat's quiet engine after tying it off. He doesn't bother storing it because we will be using it for shore runs in the coming days.

"How'd it go?" I asked him.

He wipes the sea spray off his grizzled face and yawns. The man has been up all night long, just like we guys have. "Good, boss. No problem. The

French girls are gone. They took the money, said thank you, and disappeared."

Good, good. Just how we planned it. We don't need complications, not at such an early stage.

Those could come later.

CHAPTER THREE

ABBY

WHY IS MY BED MOVING?

I lift my head from a pillow and squint against the blinding light pouring in the windows. On the other side of the thick glass is water. Lots of water.

Apparently, I spent the night on a boat. Not the Airbnb in Madrid where I'm supposed to be, and not the Airbnb in Ibiza where I'm *not* supposed to be, but on a boat owned by strangers.

One of whom gave me the best orgasm of my life.

I look around the bedroom. It seems pretty big for a boat, not that I've been on many, but it's definitely bigger than I would have expected. The bed is sprawling, king-sized I'm pretty sure, and faces a widescreen TV built into the wall.

Do people really go out on yachts and sit in their rooms watching movies?

On the side of the wall with the windows, there are two chairs that look like they swivel so you can either face them to look at the water, or turn them around and watch the TV. There is a seating area with a sofa, a small bar, and mini-fridge. It's all decorated in the dark colors that men seem to like so much, with rich wood paneling on the walls, and thick, plushy carpet.

Not that different from my dad's house, to be honest.

The most interesting thing is that I'm alone. Surrounded by utter silence.

I'm happy to be waking up by myself. I'm not complaining. But I'm pretty sure that since Bogdan and I messed around here, this must be his room.

So where is he?

I jump back into the jeans and skimpy shirt the girls gave me in case anyone barges in, and start opening doors, looking for a bathroom. A room like this surely has its own, right?

The first door I open leads to a large closet, the kind you find in celebrity magazines with built in shelves and dressers and perfect lighting.

The next door is locked. Interesting.

And the last door—bingo!

I pee and freshen up, using an unopened tooth-brush I find in the vanity. These guys probably keep a supply for all the girls they lure back to the boat. I do my best to pull my wild hair into some sort of knot on top of my head, splash a little water on my pits and vajayjay, and take a deep breath.

Time to make my appearance.

Hopefully I can just say thank you for the good time, get back to the Airbnb, and get the hell out of here. The sisters might have booked our flights, but I have my confirmation number, so I should be cool. I may even go to the airport early and cross my fingers for an earlier flight. I had about as much fun in twenty-four hours as I can toler-ate, and while Madrid is still far from home, it's where I can relax. And return all the freaking phone calls I missed from my father. He's going to be jumping mad I didn't answer last night when he called. I'll just tell him I fell asleep early. Jet lag, yo.

Speaking of which, where's my phone?

I rifle through my jeans pockets and come up with a credit card and some euros in one pocket and my red lipstick in the other.

Must have left the phone where we were

hanging last night. I think Bogdan called it the afterdeck?

So I slowly open the bedroom door, not sure what exactly lies on the other side. The night before, when I came down here with Bogdan, it was so late and so dark he could have walked me off the side of the boat and I wouldn't have noticed until I hit the water.

I enter a hallway with several other doors I figure lead to bedrooms like the one I just came out of. I don't see a soul, so I lean my ear against a couple to figure out whether I'm the first person up. But again, silence.

Is everyone sleeping later than me?

And what time is it, anyway?

I follow the hallway to stairs I remember coming down the night before—actually, probably only a few hours ago—and find myself in a huge kitchen with a dining room just beyond. It's a gorgeous kitchen by any measure but the fact that it's a full-size one on a boat boggles my mind.

I thought boats had tiny little kitchens. Clearly, yachts are a different story.

I snag a bottle of water from the fridge and climb another set of steps, this time finally hearing signs of life.

I blink in the bright sunlight and spot the short

blond hair of Ilya, who's being poured coffee by the weird little man who seems to work for the guys.

"Good morning, Miss Abby," he says in a super-strong accent that sounds similar, but not identical to the guys'. At least to my ear.

"Oh. Um, morning," I say looking around for everybody else.

Do they know what Bogdan and I did? And where is he, anyway?

I turn toward footsteps bounding up the stairs behind me, and almost bump into Fedor, who's pulling his hair back into a ponytail. His eyes flash blue at me in the sunlight, and for a moment I forget to breathe.

For a split second, I'm sorry I'm leaving these guys. The yacht is magnificent, and these men, well, they're freaking hot. But I have to be realistic. And responsible. I pushed limits the night before. Time for reality.

"Morning, Abby. Have you met our steward, Karol?" Fedor asked, gesturing toward a seat for me.

Nice manners.

"No. I mean, we saw each other last night. But haven't really met," I say with a polite smile. I just want to get out of there. Off the boat.

Sort of.

Karol nods his head toward me deferentially. "Miss Abby, are you ready for an espresso?"

Oh god. Why do Europeans love espresso so much? It's so gross and bitter.

"Oh yes. Thank you. That would be great."

I can force a little bit of that mud down my throat if it keeps everyone from thinking I'm a total hick.

I take my seat, conveniently across the table from both guys, giving me a few more moments to admire their beauty. "Thank you for inviting my friends and me last night. It was so much fun."

Ilya nods, the overhead sun glinting off his blond hair.

I self-consciously push a bit of my own, blowing in the breeze, behind my ear, as Karol serves my espresso.

Shit. Why am I doing this to myself?

I touch the tiny cup, and it's blasting hot, which means I can hold off for a moment or two, waiting for it to cool down.

"Where's everybody else?" I ask casually.

Ilya waves away my question. "Not up yet," he says simply.

Okay, then.

I look in the distance. We're close enough to see Ibiza. Shouldn't take long to get back to shore.

"So Abby, tell us about yourself," Fedor says.

Karol sets down a huge tray of croissants and they smell so damn good I want to cry.

He notices me staring. "Please, Miss Abby, help yourself. These are fresh. *Homemade*, as you Americans say."

I force myself to acknowledge him with a smile and thanks, even though I am dying to stuff one or two of these treats into my mouth. Turns out I forgot to have dinner the night before.

I tear apart the flaky pastry like Fedor and Ilya do, and pop small bites into my mouth, chewing slowly and carefully, savoring every bite.

Not having forgotten his question, Fedor looks at me with his eyebrows raised.

Shit, wait till he finds out how damn boring I am.

"Well, I live in Miami, and am heading into my third year of college. Oh, and this is my first time in Europe."

I'm using my best small talk voice, which isn't saying much, but I really am thinking it's time to get back to shore.

"How are you enjoying your holiday?" Ilya asks.

"Spain is so magical. Such amazing food and friendly people."

We go back and forth for a while comparing notes on Madrid, the only place I've really seen so far, aside from the inside of a nightclub in Ibiza, when I figure I've been polite long enough to get the ball rolling on getting off the boat and back to shore.

Still no sign of Bogdan or the sisters, but at this point, I don't even care.

"Hey, do you think you could take me back? I... have some things I need to do," I say with a bright smile.

Fedor's and Ilya's pleasant expressions don't falter, not one bit.

"Are you hungry? Would you like some lunch?" Ilya asks. "Karol can get you anything you desire. Lunch on the island is always so crowded."

Fedor nods in agreement. "It's so nice out here on the boat. We have the best of both worlds, don't we, Ilya?"

Then he jumps to his feet. "My, my. Ilya, we have been terrible hosts. We have not even invited Abby for a swim. The water here is beautiful. You must join us."

Now they're both standing, looking at me expectantly.

"Um. No. I don't really want to swim. I don't have a swimsuit, anyway."

Fedor rolls his eyes and laughs, then walks up to me and pulls me to my feet. "Turn, darling. Please do a spin for us."

What the fuck?

I comply, and find, no surprise, that they are sizing me up.

"We have the perfect bikini for you, Abby," Ilya says. "I will just have Karol go get it—"

"Oh, it's sleeping beauty," Fedor hollers as Bogdan joins us.

He greets me with a kiss on both cheeks and runs his hand down my backside. It startles me, but I have to admit it feels damn nice.

I want to ask him where he slept, but not in front of the other guys.

Ilya claps his hands together. "Bogi, we were just about to get Abby a bikini so we can take a swim."

I hold my hands up. "Oh, no, I was just asking when we're going to shore—"

But Bogdan cuts me off. "Wonderful. That sounds perfect, a lunchtime swim. Just the thing after a late night, eh?" he asks, shooting a sly smile in my direction.

"What about the girls? We need to wake them

up, right?" I ask, getting more confused by the moment.

Bogdan shakes his head no and downs the espresso Karol brought him.

Why are these guys so nonchalant? Don't they have responsibilities? Things to do? And why do they want to hang out with *me*? They could get a hundred more attractive girls on their boat.

Before I came on my trip, one of my friends told me European guys like American girls. They think we're fun, she said, and they admire our independence.

But Americans are freaking everywhere in Spain. There have got to be other women for these guys to hang with. I have neither the time nor inclination to party on a boat all day. I need to get back to the Airbnb, collect my stuff, and get to the airport.

And return my father's calls. Speaking of which.

"Hey, I was going to ask, has anyone seen my phone?"

Fedor and Ilya look at each other and shake their heads, shrugging.

"I think I saw you with it last night, right? Up here on the afterdeck?" Bogdan asks. "Let me see if Karol has seen it." He skips off down the steps.

I wander around, looking, hoping maybe it slid under something, but find nothing. And he returns a minute later, his hands empty.

Shit.

"Bogdan, when are we going back to shore?" I ask, trying to keep the edge out of my voice.

He just smiles at me, and that delicious feeling between my legs from the night before comes flooding back.

Damn him.

"Abby, you are on vacation. Now why don't you take this lovely swimsuit Ilya brought you and try it on? I'm dying for a swim."

I'm running out of patience. Quickly. "Bogdan, *when* are we going back?"

He places a hand on my arm. "The captain has other plans, Abby. I suggest you relax. Enjoy the beautiful day."

I clench my fists, hoping no one notices. It won't do to lose my shit. At least not yet.

"What other plans? What do you mean?"

This is what happens when you take a risk. Shit blows up right in your face. I never should have gotten on this damn boat. I never should have come to Ibiza. And I never should have spent five minutes of my time with those silly girls.

I should have continued to enjoy my own

company in Madrid, wandering around, seeing the sites, and eating good tapas.

What the fuck was I thinking?

Dad will be sick with worry, and when I do get back in touch with him—if my goddamn phone ever resurfaces. He'll be beyond furious. He'll demand that I come home, which he can do since he funds the debit card I've been using, and he won't let me out of his sight again until it's time to return to school.

I'm fucked. So royally fucked.

I snatch the swimsuit out of Ilya's hands and slam it down on the table that Karol just cleared and is now setting cocktails on.

"Enough with the swimsuit. I don't want to swim," I say firmly. "I don't want a cocktail. I want to go back to shore."

Bogdan presses his lips together and rubs his forehead, glancing sideways at the other guys.

What the fuck, dude?

I push past him, shoulder chucking him as hard as I can. "I'm going to find the girls. They cannot be sleeping still."

This is crazy and I don't like it one bit. If I want to be ferried back to the island, I expect them to honor my request. I have my dad to answer to. I didn't sign up to hang out on a freaking yacht all day.

And that night club where this shit all started. Yuck. I didn't even have a chance to tell the girls that when I went to the ladies' room, every other stall was full of people having sex. I can understand getting some vacation dick. But I never expected it to be so goddamn in my face.

I look out over the water to Ibiza. Definitely too far to swim. Fuck.

"I wouldn't bother if I were you," Bogdan says in a quiet voice. "Looking for the sisters."

"What? Why?" I snap.

Fedor rounds the table and puts a firm hand on my shoulder, pushing me back into my seat. "You won't find them, Abby."

My heart pounds and tears flick my eyes. But I don't want to cry in front of these guys. I misheard them, right? I am overreacting. Nothing to worry about.

Right.

"What do you mean I won't find them?" I finally ask.

"You won't find them, Abby, because they are not here."

CHAPTER FOUR

ILYA

"TOO BAD WE could not keep the French girls instead of this one."

What were their names? Did they ever tell us?

"Ilya, you had one night with... one of them," Fedor says. "Do not be a greedy bastard."

He never learned their names, either.

Fedor slaps me on the back like he's sympathizing. But, of course, he doesn't give a fuck. Not about me and my carnal needs, nor about the pretty girls who actually turned out to be pretty good company—both in bed and out. Too bad we had to send them away right after we fucked them. I would have liked to bet Fedor a thousand euros we could get them kissing each other. Maybe more.

Yes, I am a perverted fucker that way. Sometimes my deviant soul shocks even my friends. But fuck, what guy doesn't want to get it on with two hot sisters?

It would have been alright to have them hang around longer, maybe even as long as a week, or at least until I tired of them. I could have fucked them in every position, in every nook and cranny of the boat, given that much time. And I have no doubt they would have leapt at the chance to stick around, had we extended an invite. What girl wouldn't want to spend a week on a yacht with three virile men? But it was not to be, much as I might have liked it.

We had other, more important things to attend to.

Our current guest, while lovely in her own quiet, serious way, is not the same kind of fun. *C'est la vie.*

You can't have everything.

Just *almost* everything.

Which might make me sound like a greedy fuck. But I don't care. When you grow up like I did, not knowing where your next scrap of bread would come from, and not knowing which of your crazy parents was going to beat the shit out of you on any given night, you end up with a funny relationship to expectation.

First, there's a period in your life when you expect nothing. You know there's nothing coming your way. Except perhaps, a new shit sandwich.

Then, years pass. Though no easy feat, you've made something of your life. You've crawled, scraped, and run over everyone and everything in your way. But you've arrived. You have respect. You have things. You have power.

And no one will ever hurt you again.

I didn't get where I am by hoping life would throw some crumbs my way. By sitting on the sidelines, waiting my turn. By letting others go ahead of me because I'm nice. Oh, fuck no. I took life by the balls and shook out of it everything I wanted and then some. I deserve it for all I went through growing up. I am *owed* that shit. In fact, I am *still* owed a fuck ton of mea culpas from the universe. There's little I won't do to get what I want. The guys think I'm a sick fuck. They are probably right.

So sue me for being bummed the French girls are gone. But today, business is more important. Bogdan, Fedor, and I know this.

"Where did she go, the young woman?" Karol asks when he brings lunch.

Dammit, I wanted to get a swim in before eating. Hanging out on the yacht is great and all, but there isn't a lot one can do for exercise. We do have a Peloton, and I have dragged it up to the afterdeck on occasion, but it's boring as fuck to pedal and not go anywhere.

If Abby hadn't been giving us the third degree, followed by her freak out over the French sisters, I would have gotten my swim in.

Fedor waves downstairs, toward the direction of the cabins. "She is below deck looking for her friends."

Karol's eyebrows rise, and his forehead breaks into a mosaic of wrinkles. None of us knows exactly how old he is, but he helped raise Bogdan's father, so we know he's old as fuck. "She does not know what is going on?"

No, she doesn't. Although the time to tell her is drawing near. Like a goddamn speeding freight train. She'll be back up here on the afterdeck as soon as she searches all the cabins and comes up empty. The shit will hit the fan.

That's the way it always is. And we're ready.

"No, Karol, we have not told her. Speaking of

which, how did it go when you took the girls back to shore?"

He gives us what I call the 'Slavic shrug,' which he uses to answer most questions, pressing his lips together until they form an upside-down smile, and bringing his upturned palms to the level of his ears.

"It was fine," he assures us. "I gave them each their five hundred euros and instructions for what to do with Abby's things. They accepted the money with much happiness and smiles. As soon as we reached the dock, they were gone. I did get their names though, in case we need to... get in touch someday."

He holds up their French ID cards, which he must have lifted when Fedor and I were having our way with them. That's going to fuck them up a bit, but they can deal with it. They'll just assume they lost them partying.

"Good man," Fedor says, patting him on the shoulder.

"How long will you keep this woman, this Abby?" Karol asks.

It's a good question. Hopefully, no longer than necessary.

Bogdan slaps him on the back. He grew up with Karol and knows his every quirk. "Do not worry,

Karol, we will make sure you get to see her in her bikini at least once."

Karol's crinkly face beams. "She is lovely, no? Simple, but lovely. Not like Russian girls, with all that makeup." He gestures toward his face, as if he were running a paintbrush over it.

"Hey, is someone going ashore?" Fedor suddenly asks, frowning and cocking his ear toward the starboard side of the boat.

We're quiet for a second, until we identify the tender's engine grinding and turning over. But whoever's messing around with it sounds like they have no freaking idea how to start a small boat. They're going to kill the starter.

What the fuck?

"Karol, didn't you already go ashore for provisions?" I ask.

He nods slowly.

"Holy shit. Do you think..." Bogdan starts to say.

But he needn't finish. We're all thinking the same. Annoyance rises in my chest, followed by anger, only made worse when Fedor starts laughing so hard he can barely breathe. He thinks everything is fucking funny.

"She's in the tender," he gasps, doubling over. "She thinks she can get away—"

Bogdan and I run down the stairs and out the starboard door. Just as I expected, there's Abby, frantically turning the key in the tender's ignition, unable to get it started.

I have to admit, as pissed as I am, it is kind of funny to see. Poor girl. Even if she did get the thing started and figured out how to operate the throttle, which is highly unlikely, she hadn't untied it from the yacht.

Small but important details.

"Don't come near me!" she screams, pointing at Bogi and me.

We stop and watch, waiting for her next move. Might as well have a little fun. I cross my arms and tap my foot just to be a dick. Bogi looks up at the sky like he's planning how to spend the rest of his day.

"Abby, that's not going to work. Please get back on the yacht," I say calmly.

Eyes wide with fear, she looks around frantically, perhaps for a weapon, but comes up empty. "You… you have to take me back to shore. I will not be kidnapped." She glances back at the island, much too far away to swim to.

No more leaving the key in the tender. I'll have to make sure the crew is clear on that.

But she's not as green as she seems. Watching

Bogi and me, she throws the line off the cleat, releasing the tender from the yacht. It floats a few feet away, bobbing gently in the calm waters.

Hardly the dramatic escape she's hoping for.

Whatever. She's free now. If 'free' is floating around on a boat you can't operate.

Bogdan sighs and looks at me. "Do you mind?" he asks. "Or should we call the crew to go get her?"

I shake off my polo shirt and drop it on the deck. "No. I was going in for a swim, anyway."

He nods his thanks and I dive into the water.

I find this part of the Mediterranean to be chilly, which is odd for someone coming from Russia. I swam in cold water my entire life, but anymore all I really like are the warm waters of the Caribbean. But it is refreshing, especially after my late night with the insatiable French girl.

I only need to swim a few strokes to reach the tender, which Abby stands on like a fortress she's prepared to defend. She grabs a pole used to fish things out of the water and wields it like a weapon as she moves to the far side of the boat. I arrive at the back of it and pull the ladder down so I can board. I'm out of the water seconds later, dripping wet, and it's not lost on me that she's looking me up and down while I push wet hair back off my forehead.

"Put that down, Abby. Come on. Let's get back to the yacht for lunch. Karol has made a very nice shrimp salad."

But she's having none of it. I approach her and she takes a swing with the pole. Even if she manages to hit me, it won't do a thing. In fact, it's all I can do to not laugh out loud. I'm a jerk but not that big of a jerk. But I smirk. There's no avoiding that.

"What's so funny?" she screams.

Busted.

"*You* are, darling. Has anyone ever told you how hot you are when you are mad?"

This makes her falter. I suspect she doesn't get many compliments. Which is a shame. She really is quite lovely, and Bogdan did alert us to how suitably she responded to him when they were alone in his bed.

"*Zolotse,*" I say, "you are not going anywhere. So, let's just return to the ship."

I approach her slowly so as not to scare her, although I'm really not sure why. If she's afraid, she'll just have to get over it. And as I get nearer, her shoulders relax until they're slumping.

She has surrendered.

"Sit down," I say, taking the pole from her and returning it to its place. I start the tender and direct it back to the yacht. One of the crew is waiting there, so I throw him the line.

"Was it worth it, Abby?" I ask, helping her aboard. I shouldn't be a shit, but I'm in the mood to taunt. Just a little.

"Fuck off," she spits, yanking her arm out of my hand.

She's mad. I can't blame her. But she needs to accept her situation. And I plan to help her do just that.

"Abby, do you think you can behave like a grownup and have lunch with us, or do I need to take you to your room to punish you?"

Stiffening, she narrows her eyes at me. "You wouldn't dare."

So predictable.

I lunge for her before she can react and I throw her over my shoulder. She screams and wriggles, reaching for something, anything, to keep me from carrying her off, but I'm moving too fast for her to get ahold of anything.

I'm trying to keep my cool, but her thrashing and screaming starts to piss me the fuck off. She's already kicked me in the mouth, and I can taste the blood from my bottom lip.

When we get to my room, I lock the door. She looks around like a caged animal, but I suspect she knows she can't get out. "You have been a bad girl, Abby," I say, moving toward her while she's backing away.

Goddamn, I love this shit.

"Wh… what do you want with me? What did I do? Why am I here? Why are you doing this to me?"

She really is as naïve as she acts. Fuck all.

"Please let me go, Ilya," she says, her voice cracking. "I did nothing to deserve this."

She has a point. But that point has no impact on her situation.

I wave away her concerns. "Take down your pants."

Her mouth drops open. Of course, she's not going to make this easy. Which, is exactly why I want to do what I'm about to.

She backs into the wall. "Wh… what?" she asks.

"Bad girls get punished. Now you can take down your pants and bend over, or I can call Bogi and Fedor in here and they can do it for you."

I stand so close I can feel her warm breath. "Do it," I say in a whisper.

She looks down and after a moment, begins to unbutton the top of her jeans. The quiet metal-on-metal of an opening zipper follows, and she pushes her jeans below her ass.

I finally look down at her taut stomach and laugh to myself when I see her ugly panties.

Why am I not surprised?

But her nerdy librarian knickers are actually hot as fuck, and my semi-hard dick springs completely to life.

Maybe this will have to be more than a spanking.

"Very good. Now turn around and put your hands on the arms of that chair."

She glares at me one last time before she faces away, her lips trembling and her eyes shining with tears.

I slip her plain white panties below her ass cheeks, and lightly smack her behind. Then, I switch to the other cheek and deliver a few whacks. Even though I'm going easy on her, she jumps every time I touch her.

Jesus, wait till she gets a real spanking.

Whack.

I deliver a big on one her left ass cheek.

Whack.

And even it out by delivering one to her right cheek.

I run my hand over her burning, red flesh, then pull her around and to me. I need to see her eyes to really know what effect I am having.

And to my surprise, she stifles a sob, then presses her head against my chest.

Well, well. I thought she might be naughty underneath it all, and it turns out I am right.

I hook a finger under her chin to raise her face and use my thumb to wipe away the tear on her cheek. She's still breathing hard from the spanking, and her lips are plump and moist.

"*Krasotka*," I whisper, and lower my mouth to hers.

To my delight, she willingly kisses me back.

I lead her to the bed, where I remove the rest of her clothes, and step back to admire her small, puffy breasts and shaved pussy. I part her legs to see more, and she moans lightly.

Ah, the redemptive power of sensuality. It is a salve for so many woes.

But before I can part her legs further to see what is mine, she raises her head.

"Why am I here, Ilya? I did nothing."

"That may be true, *malishka*, but with a father like yours, what do you expect?"

CHAPTER FIVE

ABBY

Before I can ask any more questions, Ilya pulls his swim trunks far enough down to free his cock, holding it by the base. I have so many questions. So many worries. And I am so confused.

But I want to get away from all that, at least for a moment. And I know exactly how.

I prop my ass on the edge of the bed, sitting up. Acknowledging my willingness, Ilya moves closer, aiming for my mouth. I grip him, and after tasting the precum on his tip, dive down on his cock, taking as much as I can, nearly until I gag.

I love giving head. I have since the first time I tried it.

I know people think I'm some sort of uptight prude. But just because I don't shake my tits and ass for the world to see, wear a face full of makeup, or act like a party girl, doesn't mean I don't know how to have some fun.

Maybe I just do it differently from other people.

And while I still have no goddamn idea why I am stuck on this boat, Ilya is about to find out it's his lucky goddamn day.

With a hand firmly holding his balls, I take him all the way to the root. He tastes of the salty Mediterranean, fresh and clean, and my initial draw causes him to mini-convulse. I run my tongue over and around his head, hard and bulbous in my mouth. Spittle runs down my chin and my eyes water.

I love it.

A tingle washes over me until I shiver. My free hand finds the hungry spot between my legs, and I'm soaked like I knew I would be, my cunt puffy, my clit hard and protruding. As I slide Ilya's cock in and out of my mouth, I slide two fingers inside myself, my favorite way to get off, pleasing both of us at the same time.

But he abruptly pulls out, stepping back to see

my mouth hanging open, my cunt stuffed with my fingers.

"Knees," he says. "On your knees."

With his hands on my hips, he positions me facing away, kneeling on the edge of the bed. His cock, still wet from my mouth, slams into me so hard I brace myself against the bed to keep from flying across it.

And the sensation is so delicious, being stretched, being filled, it's like everything in the world is perfect, nothing is wrong, nothing ever *was* wrong, and nothing ever *will be* wrong. All I feel, as pure pleasure surges through my veins, somehow, incredibly, even to the end of my hair, is happiness. The kind of happiness I only ever feel when I'm doing *this*.

It's my secret. And now Ilya knows it. Bogdan learned it last night.

He pumps and pumps, growling loudly enough, I think, for everyone on the boat to hear, not that I care. His fingers hold my hips so tightly I know there will be marks later, and I don't care about that, either.

And I am grateful, although I won't be thanking him. He deserves no credit. He is just a hard cock that happens to be in the right place at the right time. I will try to get away again, no doubt about it, but while I'm here, these men will make me feel good.

I come with a screaming orgasm, my pussy contracting, milking Ilya's thrusts for all they're worth. I buck back against him to show him I can take it, my head flipping until hair's in my eyes and mouth and I can't see. The room reeks of salt water and sex, the two going together so well, as if they're made to happen side by side, the perfect complement to each other. I don't know what the fuck is going on, why I'm on this damn boat, what happened to the sisters, or what the hell Ilya meant about my father, but for a few moments it doesn't matter, for a few moments I just want a break from the madness of everything happening around me.

Problem is, it doesn't last forever. Ilya comes with a growl and when he attempts to gently lay me down on the bed, I don't fall for it and push him the hell away. I know he wanted to get his rocks off just like I did. No need to pretend it was anything more.

"Are you okay, *malishka*?" he asks, pulling his swim trunks back on.

I head to the bathroom to clean up, and most importantly, catch the cum starting to run down my leg. I pause in the doorway.

"I'm fine, Ilya. But can I ask a question?"

One of his eyebrows rises as he tries to antici-
pate what I might be asking.

"What the hell does *malishka* mean?"

He drops his head back and roars with laughter. "Oh, Abby, you are funny. It means baby girl.
Malishka. Baby girl."

Oh. Okay. Sort of trendy, but I'll take it.

He leaves and I jump in the shower, happy to
find it's fresh water. I was worried it might be
salty, but I guess on a boat like this, you get all the
creature comforts. That is, if someone doesn't take
away your phone.

Yeah, I know my phone didn't 'go missing.'
Those guys must think I'm an idiot. They have my
phone somewhere on this boat, and I plan to
find it.

Now that my post orgasm glow is being
washed down the drain, fear creeps back into my
consciousness, and I begin to worry—one of my
super powers. I'm not proud of it. But shit is what
it is.

What did Ilya mean about my father? *With a
father like mine, what do I expect?*

My dad's a successful businessman. He's fairly
well-off. Not rich—he doesn't have a yacht or
anything like that—but he does okay, and we live

comfortably. We take vacations where we aren't limited to car trips but actually fly on airplanes. I know not everybody gets to do that.

We are really not wanting for anything.

So, are they holding me for ransom? Are they hitting my dad up for money? Why? They seem to have way more than he does.

But maybe that's how they got this boat and whatever other things they have. Extort people for whatever they can get. Guess it all adds up after a while, and *poof!* one day you have a big fucking boat.

Well, Dad will pay whatever they want without delay. I know he will. He'll do anything for me. I mean, he's a needy pain in the ass, but the man loves me. After all, he's the one who stepped up to the plate when my mom bailed on us. He had to be both parents.

If only I'd gone with the DJ who wanted to show me his booth. I probably wouldn't be here right now. He had, after all, warned me to be careful. That Ibiza was bright and shiny on the surface, but it could be dangerous to a girl who hadn't been around a whole lot.

Like me.

And the French girls. What happened to them? Where did they go? Are they okay? Did they make it back to the Airbnb? Home to France?

If so, why aren't they helping me? What did they do with my passport and other stuff?

Why did they abandon me?

They mustn't have had a choice.

I have no way to contact them, except via the email they used to send me my plane ticket. Not that I have a phone to contact them with anyway.

While my head is spinning with a thousand possibilities, there's a knock on the bedroom door. I pull on a robe hanging in the bathroom.

"Come in," I call.

At least they know how to knock.

It's Karol, their gnome-y little minion, with a tray of food—a sandwich and what looks like ice tea.

"Miss Abby," he says, shuffling over the carpet, "you missed lunch, and I thought you might be hungry."

He sets the tray down on a small table by the window, which, ironically, holds a beautiful view of Ibiza in the distance.

It's like the universe is giving me the big middle finger.

Thanks!

"Thank you." I take a big swig of the tea.

He smiles. "I know Americans like their ice tea. It is good, yes?"

So good. And unsweetened, just how I like it.

"Mmmm, thank you." It is strangely comforting to taste something so familiar.

Karol makes to leave, but I stop him.

"Hey, um, Karol. What's going on here? Can you help me?" I ask, hoping that, for some reason, the man might take pity on me.

After all, he's not one of the guys. He's just their bitch.

He looks at me, his expression no different than it was a moment ago when he was kindly offering me food. "No, Miss Abby. I cannot help you."

A lump builds in my throat at the coldness in his statement. "Karol, what should I do?"

"Accept it, Miss Abby. Just accept it."

CHAPTER SIX

FEDOR

"UNLESS YOU WANT to die young, do not even think about it."

Does this American girl think we're stupid? And that with her spoiled girl 'street smarts' she can outwit three Russian gangsters?

Americans watch too many fucking movies. They're clueless. About everything. It's baffling to me. How did they ever become the world power they are, aside from winning the Cold War just because they had money and the USSR was broke?

One might expect this woman, this Abby, to be in a better mood. She just had her brains fucked out by Ilya, and yet, when she comes up for cocktails and then dinner, she's brooding and silent, glowering at anyone trying to start a conversation with her.

I do want to know more about her, if just out of morbid curiosity. What kind of woman does a crook like her father raise? Is she just like him? Or has she been sheltered, with no idea of his business dealings? And moral failings? And lack of character?

The more time she spends aboard the boat, the more certain I am she has no idea what her father does to put a roof over their heads, nor how many people he fucks over to do it.

Unfortunately for him, he's recently gone too far, and it's time to pay. He's politely been asked to rectify his mistakes, but he refuses. And this refusal puts him at the top of what I call our 'shit list,' an American saying I love so much. So, to teach him the error of his ways, convince him to right his wrongs, and let him know our faction will not be fucked with, we've taken hold of his most precious possession. His daughter.

Unless he's a total idiot, he'll stop infringing on our territory without delay. Abby will be sent home, and everyone will be happy.

Well, maybe except for her father.

Of course, Abby knows none of this. *Yet*. I'm a

big believer in 'need to know,' another lovely American saying. All she needs to understand for now is that she's on our boat for an unknown period of time, and that if she behaves, we'll treat her well.

Very well.

Fuck, I wish I'd been treated a fraction as well as she's already been, when I was a prisoner during my military service. But I'm not the kind of person people cut slack for. I still have scars to prove it.

I have to say, Abby's earlier escape attempt was funny as hell. Poor little fool. She had no fucking idea what she was doing, and yet she gave it a try anyway. Can't fault someone for that. In fact, I'm kind of impressed. She was out of the tender and back on the goddamn boat so fast, Bogdan hadn't even finished his first scotch of the day.

And if Ilya was true to form, she got her nice little ass spanked for her trouble.

But we haven't broken her yet, as evidenced by her behavior—not only is she just picking at her food in silence, but she's also clearly looking around, casing the place to see if there are any other ways to get off the boat and back to the island. She needn't be so impatient, though. She will get off the boat eventually. Just not until we are ready.

The sooner she accepts her predicament, the easier her life will be. She can make a little vacation out of being here if she just gives it a chance. At least she's not been thrown in a damp, dark basement teeming with rodents, like I was when I was her age.

Our lives will be easier too, once she settles in. Because of today's escape attempt, we'll be locking her in her room overnight rather than giving her free run of the place. That shit is a pain in my ass. I'm not down with babysitting.

"Put the fork down," I sigh.

Bogdan and Ilya are watching her too. Nothing gets past us. She will learn that quickly.

If she thinks she can stab one of us with her goddamn fork, she's not as smart as I think she is.

Say she does manage to drive her fork through someone's hand, all the way through to the table below. What the hell will she do next? Take control of the boat and return to Ibiza?

Come on, honey.

She can't possibly think that would work.

I reach over, take her fork out of her hand, and lay it back on the table on the left side of her plate where it had been set.

For Christ's sake, woman.

Her nostrils flare. "Are you going to tell me

what I'm doing here? Or did you just need a new sex slave?" she asks, her chin high to show how bad ass she is.

"*Zolotse*," Bogdan begins, "you've seen how easily women flock to our boat. Do you really think we need to coerce someone to have sex with us? You're smarter than that. I know you are."

She stiffens at his patronizing tone but says nothing. Just continues looking at us expectantly.

Oh, what the fuck.

"Abby, your father, Mr. Madden, has… broken the rules of engagement. He needs to make good on his mistakes," I say.

She frowns like that's the most ridiculous thing she's ever heard. "What?" she scoffs. "My father is a businessman. He doesn't deal with men like… you."

Poor thing. She has so much to learn. And she's not going to like what she does learn.

"Your father conducts business with all sorts of people, including those of us who control large territories. He has made the mistake of breaching ours. Unfortunately, he has to be taught the hard way that sort of behavior is not tolerated. Especially by us."

She laughs through her nose, unwilling or unable to accept the truth.

"Abby," Ilya says, "of course you think your dad is a good guy, as every daughter should. But you don't know everything about him."

She shakes her head violently. "No. *You* don't know. I'm joining his transport company after I finish college. I've worked there every summer, and he's promised to make me a partner in a few years. It's all set."

"Abby, if your dad doesn't clean up his shit, he won't be around in a few years."

She covers her mouth like someone hit her, and stifles a sob. "Is that why… I am here? If he doesn't do what you want, you are going to kill me?" Her voice breaks and tears trickle down her cheeks.

It's not easy to learn your dad is a crooked fucker. But seriously. She worked there every summer and had no idea what was going on?

I have to say I'm impressed with Madden's operation. Very discreet. Very smooth. We could all learn from that.

Her shoulders shake from her sobs, and I admit, I am tempted to take her into my arms for comfort. She seems like a sweet kid and shouldn't have to answer for the sins of her father. But it happens all the time with guys like Madden. She'll be cleaning up his messes for as long as he's alive, and probably for a long time after.

Comforting her isn't the only reason I want to take her in my arms though, truth be told. She's different. Beautiful and elegant, without even trying. Those French girls couldn't hold a candle to her with their over-the-top efforts to attract men.

A little mystery is the real aphrodisiac. A little restraint. A little coyness.

Fuck, I should write a book for women about what men want. Which is such a dick thing to say.

But I've seen the way she looks at the three of us. I know we're not bad-looking guys. We've been known to attract what I'll call female attention. And speaking for myself, I find Abby equally appealing.

I know I shouldn't act on it, but for fuck's sake, Bogdan and Ilya already have, the fuckers. There's no way I'm denying myself, that is, if she's wiling.

I don't force myself on anybody.

I take a final bite of the incredible lamb chops Chef prepared, finishing just as Abby really starts losing her shit. I mean, sobs, gasping for air, beet-red face, snot running from her nose. All of it. And I know just what to do to calm her down.

I stand up and extend my hand. "Come," I say.

I DON'T WANT Abby to think I'm a monster. I don't know why. I usually don't give a shit what people think about me. But there's something about her I can't put into words, which I've never been good with anyway, so it's no surprise.

"Come on, *zolotse*," I say quietly when we're in my room.

This is when I wish I could draw a hot bubble bath for her. But we don't have a tub on the yacht, so a nice shower will have to do.

I take her into my bathroom, and ease off her clothes. Her crying has slowed somewhat—she can at least breathe without gasping now—but her face is distorted and bright red, and when she wipes away the nonstop tears, her hands shake. I turn the shower on and guide her under the stream of water, remove my clothes, and join her.

Because we're on a boat, the shower is tight. But that's a good thing, because she turns and buries her face in my chest. I make sure the water is keeping her warm while I softly sing her a Russian folk song, the same one my *babushka* used to sing to me.

While she faces me, I take shampoo and lather up her hair, making sure to keep it out of her eyes, and I run my fingers through her curls to get it all out. Then I rub soap over her, slowing when I get to her breasts.

I turn her to face away and press my hard cock into her ass crack. My touch has calmed her, her shaking has stopped, and she lets the shower water run down her face to wash away her tears.

I rinse the soap from my hands and run them over her slick, wet skin until I reach her core. Pressing a finger between her pussy lips, I find she's wet, and not just from the shower. Dipping a finger inside her lets me know she's as turned on as I am.

I move my finger back to her clit, now hard and erect, and make slow circles with two fingers. She immediately relaxes into my embrace, dropping her head back on my chest, moving her shoulders in rhythm to my strokes.

A small whimper escapes her lips. She reaches for the grab bar on the wall, which gives her purchase. Now she can move her hips, and she begins to grind against my hand.

Fucking A, this woman is hot and I'm all too happy to give her just what the doctor ordered. Her fingers whiten on the grab bar as her grip tightens, and she convulses lightly while she moans. I gradually remove my fingers from her clit while she comes down from her orgasm and guide her out of the shower into a thick, fluffy towel. I dry every inch of her slowly and carefully, and when I look up from her feet, she's looking down on me with a small smile, and it's one of the most beautiful fucking things I've ever seen.

CHAPTER SEVEN

ABBY

"WOULD you like some more ice tea, Miss Abby?"

My heart jumps into my throat, and I take a deep breath to calm myself. Goddamn that Karol, always creeping around the boat, turning up everywhere. Just when I'm relaxing, really getting into my book or whatever it is I'm doing, it never fails. It's like the guys told him to keep an eye on me.

Which I have no doubt they did. But does he have to be so freaking diligent?

"That would be great, Karol, thank you," I say, partly to give the man something to do. I am up to my eyeballs in ice tea, but I want to stay on his good side.

If he has one.

With the guys gone—I think it's been a week now?—he seems a little lost. I guess at times such as this, he could usually go ashore and do whatever he feels like. But because I'm here, he's stuck with me.

There's not a lot to do on a yacht, but I have come up with a little routine, or as much of a routine as I can put together. I get up in the morning, ride the Peloton, take a swim around the boat a couple times—someone from the crew always watches to make sure I neither drown nor attempt to swim back to shore—and then sun myself for a bit on the bow of the boat. I read for a while, then hang out in the kitchen with Chef, who gives me stuff to do, but barely speaks to me.

In fact, aside from not much more than yes/no answers, no one talks to me. I've tried chatting up all five members of the boat's crew, and none of them wants anything to do with me. It's like I have some sort of highly contagious disease. If I need something, someone gets it for me, but anything requiring more conversation than *yes, Miss Abby*, or *no, Miss Abby*, gets a shrug and a smile.

Every couple days, Karol makes a trip to shore

in the tender—never with me, of course—and comes back with supplies that the crew unloads and puts away. I really only pay attention to the food, which Chef always manages to turn into something amazing. Seriously. If I don't watch it, I'm going to be sending Karol ashore to get me new clothes one size larger.

I have asked, and asked again, if I could go make the trip with him. The answer is always no. And with the guys gone, I am getting no information about what's going on with my father. I can't imagine what's taking so long. Whatever is it the guys are demanding of him—something about territory, I've never really gotten the full story—I'd think would be well underway.

When I ask Karol when the guys will be back, he just says 'soon.' And will anyone tell me where they've gone? Hell no.

Another boat cruised by us pretty closely the other day, close enough to stop and talk and say hi. I thought of asking them for help, and just as I was about to, one of the crew appeared on deck and told them to be on their way.

How fucked is that?

So, I am a prisoner in a place most people would die for. A floating prison. Pure luxury from top to bottom. One of the guys even had some expensive designer clothes sent from the mainland to the island for me, which Karol picked up on one of his trips ashore. 'Resortwear,' they call it. Lots of white linen. It's actually quite nice. It's nothing I ever, in my wildest imagination, thought I would wear. But I kind of like it.

And even better, there were bags and bags of stuff in addition to my white linen collection. A bunch of pairs of Levi's in both dark and light washes, all styles of tops, lace undies, Veja sneakers, and even a couple dresses I might actually wear.

If I don't get out of here first.

Still, it's pretty amazing they got my sizes right. They even asked if I wanted someone from a salon to come out to the boat and do my hair and nails.

It's all so freaking weird.

Anything I want, it is mine.

Except freedom. Except the ability walk down the street, enter a restaurant, or even call my dad.

To go home and go back to school, live my life, continue my studies. Yeah, those are the little things that are flat-out off the table.

So, I'm working on a nice tan, I've read about a book a day, and I'm trying to teach myself to draw with the pencils and sketch pad Karol got me in town.

So stimulating!

Since I am minus my phone, the sketch pad has served another important purpose. I've drawn a calendar so I can keep track of the days.

And the guys have been gone for a week now.

What the fuck?

I just woke up one morning, locked in my room. I looked out my little window and saw we were docked back in Ibiza. I pounded on the window, but none of the passersby were close enough to see or hear me. But I could see them. Happy, shiny people walking by hand in hand, in their tropical finery—linen for the gentlemen, and strappy dresses and shoes for the ladies. An hour later, the boat started moving, and Ibiza got smaller and smaller until I almost couldn't see it anymore. Someone unlocked my door and walked away. When I came out, I headed upstairs to breakfast, where the table was set for one person.

Me.

All Karol would tell me was that the guys were out of town but would be back.

I can't deny I haven't thought a couple times of throwing myself overboard and getting the inevitable over with. I don't think it would take much for these guys to kill me, and if Dad doesn't come through, I'm sure I'll end up at the bottom of some ocean.

The fact that I've messed around with them means nothing. I'm sure they'd cut me loose at a moment's notice, given enough reason.

I keep thinking back to the night at the club, and the DJ, and how the guys had chased him off. But hadn't it looked like they all knew each other?

Was it just a set up? Make the DJ look bad so the guys could come to my rescue?

And what about the French girls? Had that been a set up too? Why else would they have pushed so hard to get me to join them in Ibiza?

Was there *no one* I could trust? Shit, even my father had some bullshit going on I had no idea about.

I push my frustration into the baguette dough I'm kneading in the galley, when I hear a boat engine draw near. Chef is letting me help out, probably because he got tired of my standing there, watching him. I figure, at least I am acquiring a skill I can take home, if I ever get home. I look at Chef to gauge his reaction to the sounds, but true to form, he acknowledges nothing and just keeps stirring whatever it is he's cooking.

The footsteps and voices grow louder.

I abandon my baguette and cautiously head

toward the noise. It takes me only two steps to realize the guys are back.

I have this weird urge to run and hug them. What the hell is that all about? They're my freaking captors.

Am I coming down with some sort of Stockholm Syndrome? Only at sea?

I may want to run to them, but I do not. They don't need to see any weakness on my part. Even though I've been so lonely and bored, with no one to talk to, I can't deny I am strangely happy they're here.

At the same time, I also want to rage right in their handsome faces. Where do they get off leaving me? No communication, no goodbye, nothing. About that, I am pissed.

In fact, I'm *really* pissed.

"Where were you?" I demand, interrupting their conversation.

The three turn slowly, and goddammit, why do they have to be so gorgeous?

Bogdan, in his crisp trousers and snug polo, lowers his sunglasses to look at me. While checking me out, and with a half-smile, he nods with approval.

Ilya, his blond hair lightly gelled, wearing faded blue jeans and a collared shirt, puts his hands on his hips, the little dimple in his chin so prominent I can barely stop looking at it.

And Fedor, his hair pulled into a hipster man bun, wears his usual long-ish shorts and a buttoned linen shirt, the sleeves rolled up to show off his sexy ink.

These guys are the very definition of Mediterranean chic. If I didn't know better, I'd think they were trust fund babies from someplace like Monaco.

I'm screwed. So completely screwed.

"Well?" I snap.

Bogdan approaches me and I let him give me a kiss on the temple. "Is our *krasotka* friend a little grumpy today?" The corner of his mouth turns up, and he affectionately tucks a curl behind my ear, ignoring my obvious discontent, made only worse by yet another Russian endearment that I do not understand.

I promise myself to no longer ask for translations. I won't give them the satisfaction.

"You guys left me here. I had no idea where you'd gone or when you'd be back."

They're silent for a moment, as if truly surprised I expect anything of them.

And the truth is, I'm surprised, myself. These guys fucking kidnapped me to extort something from my father—what, I'm still not clear about. They're criminals involved in some sort of organized crime, from what I can tell, so why should I be insulted they don't treat me with any sort of consideration? How the hell else would they treat someone like me?

These guys kill people who cross them. I can hardly expect them to be models of propriety, where they inform their guest of their comings and goings.

And yet.

If I dig deep and am really honest with myself— my feelings are hurt.

I am a pathetic idiot.

How in god's name can I expect them to give a shit about me? And yet, I do.

While I'm dealing with my confusion, the guys refrain from answering any of my questions. Instead, they just point in the direction of one of the crew who joins us, setting a box on the floor in front of me. He disappears as quietly as he appeared.

"What the hell is this?" I snap.

They look at each other with a chorus of *don't know, open it,* and *don't you want to find out?*

So I lift the lid off the box and step aside in case it's something dangerous.

But it's not.

Oh god no.

It's a puppy. Like a baby dog type of puppy. It looks up at me from the blanket it's curled up in, where it must have been napping until I rudely awakened it, and yawns with a creaky little whine.

Something in me breaks open, and I reach into the box to pull out the squirming, pudgy tank of a baby, desperately trying to hold back tears. The puppy, which turns out to be a girl, takes one look at my face, closes her eyes, and nestles into my chest to return to her nap.

And there we have it. I'm in love.

Which was probably the plan.

"So do you like her?" Fedor asks, his light blue eyes catching the sun.

I nod, mostly because I'm pretty sure my voice is about to crack, but I'm also buying time to think.

Why did the guys do this for me? Why a puppy?

Are they manipulating me into submission? Do they think having her around will make me less likely to try and leave?

Poor little baby is a prisoner just like me.

But she's mine, in part because I don't trust the guys to take care of her, which means that if I do get the chance to escape, I'll have to take her with me. This complicates matters significantly.

So, I will bide my time. I will win over the guys, make them think I love life on the boat, that I never want to go anywhere else, and that I am a compliant little prisoner.

I know what I have to do.

At last, I have a plan. If the guys are going to manipulate me, I will manipulate them right back. They aren't the only ones with tools at their disposal. I have my own, and I'm ready to use them.

Even if they are my body and soul.

CHAPTER EIGHT

BOGDAN

"WHAT ARE you going to call her?"

Abby doesn't look at any of us, just keeps nuzzling the drowsy puppy.

I have to admit, she is a cute one. There's nothing like a baby Labrador.

"I don't know," she mumbles. She seems to like her gift.

No. *Correction*. She seems to *love* her gift.

"You can give her a name when you're ready," Fedor says, running his hand over the puppy's round little head. She barely moves, but her tail twitches, shaking her cute behind.

Five minutes on the boat, and that dog already

has us bewitched. Kind of like the job Abby is doing on us.

"We'll have to keep her on a leash so she doesn't go overboard," he adds. "Karol is setting up her dog bed in your room."

Abby nods and continues rocking the puppy.

Then, as if struck by lightning, she perks up with a pretty smile. "I'm going to get some sun. Anyone care to join me?"

She clearly has found at least one way to spend her days, but I am suspicious of her sudden change in temperament. She's working us. But I can work her right back.

Before Ilya or Fedor can speak up, I answer her invitation. "Hey, the guys have something to do, but I'd like to join you, Abby. Maybe we can go for a swim too."

Ilya and Fedor throw me a dirty look. Yeah, I just cockblocked them. I don't give a fuck. I want to spend some time with her and figure out where her head is. And whether she's going to be a problem.

"Great," she chirps. "I'll throw on my bathing suit."

For a moment, she looks down at the puppy, like she's not sure what to do with her, and then skips off.

"That was a dick move," Fedor says with a snort.

"Yup," I agree. "Sure was."

A minute later, I knock on Abby's cabin door and hear her cooing at the puppy. "Hey, come by my room when you're ready, okay?"

The guys and I have been away for a little more than a week, so I need a moment to settle in while Abby changes.

Back in my room, there isn't much to do. Karol beat me to it, bless him. He put all my clothes away, and the dirty ones disappeared like they always do, most likely to be returned later today or tomorrow morning.

He is amazing, that man. I trust him with my life. Sometimes I feel badly he waits on me hand and foot. But I also take care of him. He is compensated nicely, and when the day comes for him to retire, he'll want for nothing.

"Hey, sailor," Abby says, seductively leaning up against my doorjamb.

I whip around and there she is, suntanned and delicious in the white string bikini we picked up for her.

Damn if living on a boat doesn't suit this woman well. It might not be exactly what she wants at this moment in her life, but she looks like she was made for the role.

A lot of women would kill to hang out on a yacht all day, sunning themselves and relaxing, without a care in the world. No cooking, cleaning, going to the office. Shit, sounds like a good gig to me.

But not Abby. And that's what I like about her. She's not content to sit around on her ass and let someone else foot the bill. Unfortunately, that's what she has to do right now, given how difficult her dirtbag father is being.

"Damn, baby," I say, adjusting my trousers, "you look fucking awesome in that. Holy shit."

Her gaze locks with mine, and she saunters toward me while reaching behind her back. Her bikini top springs open and reveals her lovely tits, pale in contrast to her tan. She boldly stands inches from me and puts my hands on them.

I never complain when a beautiful woman takes her clothes off for me. But something about Abby's actions feels off. I can't put it into words, but her zero-to-sixty about-face, when I stop thinking with my little head, feels off.

Sure, she's a young woman and no doubt has desires. But she was scowling at me and the guys not fifteen minutes ago to the extent that if she had a knife, she might have cut one of us up. So, just because she's hot as fuck doesn't mean she can lead me around by my dick. As nice as that might be for a while.

I grab her wrists, and she freezes, the wanton look on her face dissolving into a strange combination of defiance and fear. She tries to jerk out of my grip, only stopping when she realizes her efforts are futile.

"What are you doing, Abby?"

She recovers quickly and looks down at her breasts, then back at me. "What does it look like I'm doing?" she asks coyly, pressing her hips forward against my erection.

I laugh at her. I can't help it. "I know what you're doing, Abby," I say, pressing her arms to her sides so she's standing like a mummy.

She frowns. "That's good. I mean, I should hope you know what I'm doing," she scoffs.

"No, I mean, I really know what you're doing. Coming in here and throwing yourself at me. I know the type, and you're not that type."

I know risk offending her, but I don't care. Too bad if her feelings get hurt. I want to know her motivations. Does she want to suck my dick to gain some sort of favor over her situation? Or does she really just want some nookie to bide her time here on the boat?

Maybe both?

It doesn't matter, though. I will not be manipulated, and if she thinks she can get away with shit like this, she's more naïve than I thought.

Her eyes fill with rage, clearly answering my question. It's not like I don't want to fuck the woman. I do. But I first, want to know what's motivating her to show up in my cabin, putting on a little striptease.

"*Fuck* you," she hisses.

Yeah, she doesn't give a damn about getting her rocks off.

"Whoa. What's going on here?"

I look over Abby's shoulder to see Ilya in the doorway. We never closed the door.

"Hey, man, come on in. And shut the door, will you? I don't need the entire crew enjoying the striptease Abby is about to give us."

"What?" she snaps, still trying to wriggle out of the straightjacket position I have her in.

Ilya's eyebrows rise and he turns the lock on my door with a satisfying *click*. He approaches us until he's just behind Abby, essentially sandwiching her between the two of us.

Nice.

"Now, Abby," I say slowly, "I'm going to release your arms. Ilya and I are going to sit over there in those comfy chairs. And you are going to finish the striptease you started."

I let go of her and she immediately turns and tries to run, but smacks right into Ilya, who puts his hands on either side of her face.

"*Malishka*, slow down. We're on a boat. There is nowhere to go," he says, running his fingers down her chest until he reaches her nipples.

He cups her breasts, running his thumbs over her hard points, and in spite of herself, she sighs, her shoulders rolling into a place of relaxation, releasing her urge to take flight.

Ah, Ilya. He's always got the perfect touch.

"C'mon, honey," he says softly, leading her over to the chairs. He shows her where to stand and grabs himself a seat. I am right behind him.

I take my phone and start streaming slow, sexy music to my Bluetooth speakers. Ilya waits for the show to start.

"C'mon, honey," I say. "Let's get the party started. This is not the time to pretend to be shy."

"What if I don't want to?" she asks, now playing the brat.

Damn. She has all sorts of tricks up her sleeve.

Ilya and I look at each other. "You don't want to know, *malishka*," he says impatiently.

A pink blush washes over her face, which gives me one of the hardest erections I've ever had. I don't know what it is about making her realize who's boss, but it's fucking hot.

Not to mention fun.

Having accepted her fate, she starts shifting her hips in time to the music. Initially, she's stiff. But when Ilya and I sit back in our lounge chairs, stretching and spreading out, she gains some confidence. She begins to run her hands over her tits, down her stomach, sliding them inside her swimsuit bottom.

Fuck yeah.

Her eyes fall closed as she runs her fingers between her legs. With her free hand, she unties her bikini at the hip and what is nothing more than a small scrap of fabric falls to the floor.

Now that she's completely nude, she really starts writhing to the music, grinding her hips with her arms in the air one moment, twisting like a snake, then alternating between playing with her tits and pushing her fingers between her bare pussy lips.

Ilya twirls his finger in the air. "There you go, baby. Turn around."

She faces away, giving us a lovely view of her curvy ass, jiggling just a teeny bit as she writhes for us.

"Bend over," Ilya says.

She looks back over her shoulder as if she didn't understand him, but to her credit, she keeps dancing.

"You heard him," I add.

So she slowly lowers her torso until her feet touch her toes, giving us a delicious view of her most private parts. From where I sit, I see her pussy glistening in the light coming through the window, and her pink asshole quivering from the air touching it.

She's divine. I look over at Ilya, and he nods back at me.

What a treasure we've found.

Who knew that when we went after Abby's dirtbag father that he'd be gifting us—intentionally or not—with such a gem of a daughter?

She starts to straighten up, but Ilya is having none of it. "Don't," he barks, getting up and walking over to her. He rubs the front of his trousers against her wet pussy, then pulls back and opens her cheeks further.

"Put your hands on the edge of the bed," he directs, walking her over.

He opens his pants, and with no preamble, stabs his dick right inside her. She shrieks and then moans, and after a couple strokes, she's pushing back against him like the horny little girl she is.

In moments, she's slamming her hand down on the bed, bucking her head, coming violently and loudly. Ilya quickly follows, driving inside her one more time and holding himself there while emptying his load.

I'll have to give him shit later for being a minute-man. But that's what happens when you're with someone like Abby. Someone so different and somehow more sexy than our usual fare.

He pulls out and tucks his dick back in his pants. Abby starts to straighten up too, but he pushes her back down.

"Your turn, brother," he says with a nod in my direction.

Goddamn right it's my turn.

As he passes me on the way back to his chair, ready to enjoy my show, he speaks quietly. "She can take it in the ass if you want it. I had two fingers in there and it drove her up the fucking wall."

Fuck me. As if my cock isn't already hard enough, I just about come in my pants. I pull myself out of a tangle of boxers and run a wet finger over her pretty little rosebud. To ensure Ilya isn't bullshitting me, I pop a couple fingers past her tight ring and find little to no resistance. My sweet Abby is ready to get fucked in the ass.

CHAPTER NINE

ABBY

I DON'T KNOW who I hate more—the guys or myself.

They've stolen from me—my vacation, my ability to get back to the States, my plans to return to school. Shit, my ability to walk down the damn street. I don't even have a freaking passport anymore.

And I hate that I *want* them, which makes me hate myself. Maybe even more than I do *them*.

How do you crave someone who's taken so much from you—unless you're a fucking weak hypocrite? I should be repulsed by them, my captors. And yet my heart pounds every time I look at their handsome, criminal faces. My breath quickens every time they touch me. And I come so fast when they fuck me, it's embarrassing.

I'm not like the other girls they're used to, like the French sisters, who only care where the next party is. They haven't spent enough time with women like me to know what to expect. And what I can do. I'm smart and I'm strong. I may not have seen much of the world thanks to my overprotective father, but I have good instincts. I can smell trouble.

These guys are trouble.

And now I'm in trouble.

What the hell has my father done to alienate them so? He's not my favorite person in the world, but he's not a bad man. He raised me singlehandedly. He could have afforded help, like a nanny or housekeeper, when my mother took off. But he wanted to do it all himself. Did he always do it right? Of course not. But I turned out okay.

Bottom line is, I hate these three men. I hate that I want them, and I hate myself most of all because of it.

I need to fight these feelings and stay mad. How the hell else will I escape? I can't become complacent, regardless of the new clothes and freaking puppy they're trying to manipulate me with. I have to stay on my toes. Look for opportunities to escape.

I'd even thought briefly about whether, given the opportunity, I'd kill them. I want to say I would. But the truth is, you don't know the answer to something like that until you're faced with the opportunity.

And now, Ilya and Bogdan are ravishing me, and while I shouldn't enjoy it, I'm practically begging for it like a goddamn dog in heat. I'm weak. And ashamed.

"Such a pretty little bum," Bogdan whispers next to my ear as he sets himself up behind me and bends over my back.

He's running his cockhead over my asshole, and we both know what's next.

I can't fucking wait.

I want him inside me. All the way. I want him to dive so deeply I scream. I want him to wrap his legs around my hips, get on top of me, and drill my ass until I can't walk. It will be a respite, however momentary, from my reality. I need it. Badly.

And when he pops his head inside my only slightly-prepared bottom, I screech, the burn radiating to the tips of my fingers and toes. I've done this before—not a lot, but still—and know that in seconds it will feel good. Really fucking good.

He pushes further, and I reach back with one of my hands to hold his hip to keep him from going too fast.

"You okay, baby?" he whispers, not pushing any further but pulsing in my rear end while he dislodges the hand I'm trying to control him with.

I gulp. "Yeah. Just give me a sec. Please," I gasp.

My fingers clench into fists, then open, then fist again as I throw my head on the soft bed under me. I reach to rub my clit, but Bogdan intercepts my hand and pushes it back on to the bed.

"No playing with yourself, baby. That's for me to do. If I feel like it," he rasps.

In a minute or two I'm ready and push back for more dick. Bogdan laughs with pleasure.

"So fucking hot, baby, watching my cock slide in your asshole."

He pushes harder and I grunt. We need lube, but I don't want to stop for anything. Even if it is uncomfortable.

I might like the pain.

Actually, I know I like the pain.

When did I become so self-destructive?

Ilya appears next to us, stroking a brand-new erection, like he was bored from watching us across the room. "Fucking hot, baby," he says, reaching under me to drag his finger between my cunt lips.

Did he touch Bogdan when he did that? Do these guys do stuff like that?

Ilya leaves my pussy and pushes his finger into my mouth. "Suck, *malishka*," he growls.

I lick the cream off his finger, then close my lips around it, while Bogdan pushes deeper inside. I doubt I can take all of him, and even though he's only partially up my ass, I know he likes it from his heavy breathing and moans.

A drop of spit hits my crack, and he rubs it around my asshole as if that's going to help, and pushes a little further. He stops, and pulses for a bit, then withdraws and repeats.

I'm shaking from the delicious sensation in my behind and push back to take more. I feel like a flower opening up to a new universe of pleasure as everything between my legs clenches and throbs.

"Oh god," I sputter, pushing Ilya's finger out of my face, "oh god, oh god."

I can't stop repeating myself and my entire body explodes in a violent orgasm. I pound the bed below me, bucking and thrashing to the point where I nearly throw Bogdan off. But he has my hips and isn't letting me go anywhere.

With a huge groan, he drives inside me one

more time and holds himself, his orgasm pulsing in my ass. He shudders for what seems like several minutes and, strangely, I come again. When he stops and has caught his breath, he pulls out and gets me a towel from his bathroom.

After I've cleaned up, I pull my white bikini back on. With a slightly sore bottom, I head to the bow of the boat to read and get a little sun, feeling like the sexy goddess that I am. But before I do, I check on the puppy, still sleeping in her dog bed under the watchful eye of the crew. I kiss her little head and she looks up at me, yawns, and goes right back to sleep.

She's got me wrapped around her finger already.

I hope to do the same with the guys.

"So, you know nothing about what your father does?"

I look up from my book and find the guys have joined me, casually sitting around the bow in their board shorts and sunglasses. I take a quick glance at Bogdan and wonder if he's thinking about what he just did to my ass.

"Fedor, I told you what he does," I say with a sigh.

How many times have we gone over this?

I turn back to my book in defiance, but they wait for me to answer.

I sigh again. Loudly. "He has a trucking company. He has contracts with large companies that ship a lot of stuff. He's also getting into the public sector. You know, delivering shipments for state and federal governments. I'm going to work for him after I finish college."

I go back to my book like it's the end of the conversation. But I know better.

I see Bogdan's amused, mocking expression out of the corner of my eye, which chafes the hell out of me. Fine. He knows something I don't. Whatever.

"What?" I snap.

"Well, what you should know, pretty girl," he says, tucking a long curl behind my ear, "is that we are competing for the same contracts as your father. In order to keep things fair—you know, give everyone a chance at the opportunities—we each have our own territory. Your dad, though… has turned out to be a greedy man, overstepping his bounds. Unfortunately, he's done this many times over the years. And now he's gone too far."

I sigh and flip to my back, adjusting the sunglasses and hat the guys got me to shade my face. I'm aware all eyes are on me and my skimpy bikini. I can't lie. I kind of like it. It's powerful. I've never felt sexy before.

Do I believe the guys about my dad? Well, he's an ambitious business man. I know on more than one occasion he's bulldozed people who got in his way. He brags about stuff like that to me, egocentric as he is. But I never dreamed he was either working with criminals, or doing anything as stupid as crossing them.

So maybe Dad did fuck up, without really understanding the consequences. But it's probably just a misunderstanding. He'll straighten it all out, I am sure.

"Usually we have a nice, calm conversation with your father, but lately, he's not cooperating. When that happens, we resort to more drastic... measures."

Like kidnapping a man's daughter? Is that really the only option?

"Well, when he found out you had kidnapped me, what did he say? I mean, I'm sure he'll do whatever it takes to get me home. Right?"

Instead of answering, they keep peppering me with questions.

"Where's your mom?" Ilya asks.

I scoff. Like they don't know.

I may be new to hanging out with criminals,

but I am pretty sure people like these guys knew everything about my family before they decided to 'negotiate' with my dad. I wouldn't think they'd leave much to chance, preferring to know what they're getting into, as well as the strengths and weaknesses of their adversaries.

But I'll humor them with conversation. For a while, at least.

"Mom took off a long time ago. She didn't want us anymore. She didn't want Dad and me. She didn't want to be part of a family."

Cripes, after all these years, it still hurts to say *family*.

"Where is she now?" Bogdan asks.

I shrug. "Dunno."

"That's hard," he adds, I guess to be nice.

But I don't need him to be nice. I want to know what the hell is up with my father.

"Have you been in touch with my dad?" I ask, out of patience.

The guys exchange glances, and Bogdan clears his throat. "This past week, you know, when we were gone?"

My heart thumps in my chest. Please give me some good news. "Yeah?"

"We flew to Miami to meet with your father."

Holy fuck. You could knock me over with a

feather. My heart thumps in my chest. "Wh... why didn't you tell me? Tell me you were going?"

He looks out over the water toward Ibiza. "You didn't need to know."

Anger washes over me, and I press my lips together to hold in a rage so strong it stings like poison in my veins. I want to kill these guys. I really do.

"Did you hurt him?" I ask, trying to steady my voice.

Bogdan turns back to me. "Of course not."

"H... how is he? Did you tell him about me? He must be worried sick."

Once again, the guys look at each other. If they hurt my father, so help me...

"Of course we told him we have you. He's looking into our request. We should know soon whether he will accommodate us, or continue to make foolish decisions."

"Foolish decisions? If it's a matter of getting me freed, I know he'll do anything."

Silence.

What the fuck?

Hadn't Dad warned them not to hurt me? Assured them he'd do anything he had to in order to get me back? Apologized for any mistakes he made and promise to honor their agreements going forward?

Or did he tell them to go fuck themselves, like he has so many other people?

And what does that mean for me?

———————

CHAPTER TEN

ILYA

"Jesus, that man's a prick."

I look around the galley where Bogdan, Fedor, and I sit at the kitchen table, meeting. I'll miss this place when we move on. Living on a yacht is a sweet deal, one I never dreamed I'd experience during the shitshow that was my childhood. Not enough food to go around, no heat in the winter, a drunk fuck of a father. And that's just the beginning.

I know a lot of kids in Russia had it worse than me. But that didn't mean I wasn't going to do what I had to in order to climb out of poverty. Yup, I did what I had to. I haven't always been nice. In fact, I've rarely been nice. And I have no regrets.

I can't say, however, that the shit I went through—these days people call it *trauma*—is forgotten. The goddamn mess that is my past clings to me like gum on the bottom of my shoe. I've tried a thousand times to scrape it off, but it just won't go away. Maybe someday I'll be able to accept it. That it's here to stay. It impacts every thought I have and everything I do. That's how shit like this works. You think you've left it behind, but no. Never. The gift that keeps on giving.

It keeps me on my toes. I'm always aware that with one wrong move, I could lose everything. That's what happens to people like me. So I'm always scanning my surroundings, assessing people, waiting to make a move when necessary.

It works well in this business. The moment you make a little money, get fat and happy, forget where you've come from, lose sight of the future, is the moment the next asshole in line takes it all from you.

Which brings the guys and me to our discussion of Abby's father. The man is a fool. Despite repeated warnings, he hasn't learned to stay in his lane. It's going to cost him. And he doesn't seem a bit concerned about his daughter.

In the background, Chef's cooking something amazing, some sort of paella in honor of our being in Spain and all. He's the perfect employee. Kicks ass at his job, gives us no trouble, and doesn't repeat a fucking thing he hears.

How do we know this?

His phone is bugged. All our employees' phones are bugged. It's one of the things you have to do in our line of business. No one is trusted until they prove themselves. And even then, we don't trust anybody.

"When should we tell her?" Bogdan asks.

Fedor scrapes his hand through his hair and stares at the ceiling. "The question is, *should* we tell her?"

Poor girl will be devastated when she learns that, basically, her father couldn't give a shit about her. We met with the bastard in Miami, laid everything out for him, and asked if he ever wanted to see his daughter again.

He didn't answer.

Zilch. Nothing. Nada.

Which says it all.

The fucker is entirely disinterested in his daughter's safety. Normally I wouldn't care about shit like this. Fucked up family? Not my problem. But Abby's different. She's special.

And she deserves a father who gives a shit about her.

"I say ride it out. Let's see what happens. Although she's starting to ask what's taking so long. I hate to tell her that her old man is dragging his feet," I say. "She's no idiot. She'll put two and two together and realize Daddy's a fucking loser."

"What about the villa?" Fedor asks. "Karol says it's ready for us, and I personally wouldn't mind getting off the boat."

The question is, is Abby a flight risk? Will she try and take off? She won't get far with no money, phone, or passport, but that doesn't mean she won't try. But we're all getting a little stir crazy on the boat. It would be nice to stretch our legs. Take a long walk. The yacht is amazing, but you have to get back on land at some point. We never thought we'd be on the boat for such a long stretch.

"Look," Bogdan says, "we'll tell Abby she'll be free to leave soon. And now that she has the puppy, she'll think a little harder before bolting."

I hope to god Bogdan is right. I'd hate to see Abby get hurt. As much as I like her, when it comes down to it, if we're faced with an 'us versus her' situation, she wouldn't fare well.

It's a brutal, ugly fact.

ON THE WAY to my room, I pass Abby's room and see her door wide open. The puppy is jumping all over her where she lies on the floor, licking her face. The harder Abby laughs, the more the puppy licks her.

It's a beautiful thing to see. A pretty girl playing with her puppy, laughing and rolling on the floor with the pudgy little thing.

After taking a swim around the boat, Abby must have come back in and showered. She's now wearing the cut-off white shorts and a snug little T-shirt we guys got her. As she rolls around, oblivious to my spying on her, the shirt stretches across her breasts, revealing she's not wearing a bra, and the shorts slide up on her thighs, revealing her ass cheeks, and even part of her pretty pussy.

Fuck all. I had shit to do to get ready to go ashore, but that's not happening now. I adjust the hard cock in my shorts and knock on Abby's door.

"Have you named the puppy yet?"

The dog comes running up to me and jumps on my leg. I pick her up. I can't resist.

Abby rolls over to her back and props herself up on her elbows. Goddamn if she isn't delicious. "No. She remains nameless for now."

The puppy squirms in my arms, trying to lick my face, and Abby drops her head back, laughing. "That is the cutest thing. A little puppy running roughshod over a Russian gangster," she giggles.

She's right. It is funny.

I hold the puppy at arms' length with one hand, wiping my face off with the other. "I don't know where you heard that nasty rumor, miss," I say, walking into her room and sitting on the edge of the bed.

And dammit, all I can think about is watching her take Bogdan in her ass, a scene that's going to provide me plenty of jerking pleasure for weeks to come.

I hand the puppy back to her, and she puts her in her little dog bed in the corner.

"How are you?" I ask spontaneously, and not without regret.

What the fuck kind of idiot am I? This is not the kind of conversation you have with someone you're keeping against their will.

She looks at me curiously and shrugs. She's just as surprised by my impulsvity. "What do you mean?"

I try not to stare at the nipples poking through her T-shirt.

Hell if that shirt wasn't a good purchase.

I gesture around the room. "Do you have what you need? Are you comfortable?"

She thinks for a moment. "I guess. It's my first time on a yacht. It's pretty cool. I suppose you've been on them hundreds of times."

I slowly shake my head. "You have no idea. I grew up with nothing. Less than nothing, actually."

Fuck, why was I telling her this?

"We were so poor I had to dig in the neighbor's garbage for scraps."

Her eyes grow wide as her hand flies to her chest.

This is why I don't tell people my story. I hate pity. I hate the look that settles on their faces, all but saying 'poor Ilya.'

But she says nothing. And I can't keep myself from continuing.

"There were some rough times right after the USSR collapsed. My dad didn't take it well. He was always a big drinker, like a lot of Russian men, but he just started to lose himself in the bottle."

"What happened to him?" she asks quietly.

I haven't even shared this story with Bogdan and Fedor. "He was in a bar and got in a fight, probably being an asshole. He was jumped on the way home. Stabbed."

She nods slowly, her face curious—but not

pitying. "It's incredible to know that was your life. I mean, look at you now, surrounded by such riches."

She's right. I am surrounded by riches. But the feeling of being poor will never be completely gone. Poverty is funny that way.

Abby takes a seat on the bed next to me. "Seems we both have lived through some fucked-up family shit."

I nod, remembering the story about her mother bailing.

So I take her hand and gently lay her back on the bed. I run my fingers through her wild, curly hair, and trace an outline along her temple, over her cheek, and to her mouth.

She laughs. "You're tickling me."

"Shhh," I say, brushing my finger back and forth over her lower lip, examining it like it's the first time I've seen it.

And maybe it is. I've looked at Abby many times over the past couple weeks, but I've never really *looked* at her.

Until now.

I push my finger between her lips, just to the first knuckle, and she closes around it. I push further inside her mouth, and she sucks, swirling her tongue. I slide it in and out and goddamn, I'm about to cream my pants just watching her.

I jump off the bed and in two steps am at her door, which I close with a *bang*. Then, I lower my shorts and holding my cock at the base, return to the edge of the bed, watching her part her lips just enough to moisten them with the tip of her tongue. Her nipples are so hard they're nearly tearing through her shirt and it's all I can do to keep my hands off them, but I'm holding my dick and that's my priority at the moment. And just as I expected, she scoots to the edge of the bed, digs her fingers into my ass cheeks, and pulls me in to lick the precum off my dick.

That little swipe of her tongue nearly kills me, and I push into her mouth like a man possessed. I'm thinking with my little head, which I hate because that shit is dangerous, renders a man weak, and leads to nothing but trouble.

Yet here I am.

And they call women the weaker sex? The fools who believe that are fucking idiots. There's nothing weaker than a man with a hard-on.

I watch Abby in wonder. That this girl can make me feel so good is like some sort of goddamn miracle. She opens as wide as she can and chokes a little, tears trickling down her cheeks. I want to pump her mouth harder but the last shred of self-control I have keeps me from choking her senseless.

"Such a naughty girl, *malishka*, sucking my cock like that," I say, roughing up her already-wild hair.

My legs can barely support my weight, so I grip her hair like a lifeline, and she responds by holding my ass tighter. We hang on each other, tossing in a storm of passion. Then, without warning, she spits me out of her mouth and pushes me back onto the carpeted floor of her room, straddles me, and sinks on top of my cock.

Fuck yeah.

I'm already close to coming, and now inside her pussy, my explosion is so near that my groin hurts, actually, everything hurts, but I want to get her off. With my hands on her hips, I push to meet her thrusts. Suddenly, her shoulders slump and she convulses lightly, and I am in wonder that any woman can make me feel like she does. She's so wet and grips my cock so snugly that I push up and into her one more time and she explodes, followed immediately by my ejaculation, which I leaves me vibrating from head to toe.

It's too bad she won't be with us indefinitely. I mean, we *could* keep her if we wanted to, no problem, but that gets into trafficking and that's not our thing—that's for immoral weaklings who have no other way of making money.

But maybe when she learns her father is just a low-life scum dressed up in designer rags, she'll realize the three of us are not so bad.

CHAPTER ELEVEN

ABBY

WHY BOGDAN, Fedor, and Ilya thought it was a good idea to bring a little puppy on a boat is beyond me. We're in the tender heading for shore, which I would normally be ecstatic about for obvious reasons, but the dog is a squirming little beast in my arms as I try to keep her from going overboard.

"Let me take her," Karol says, extending his wrinkled arms. She settles into him, because of course, and she starts to relax, her little nose wiggling in the breeze at all the new smells around her.

I love my furbaby, I really do, and I think the

guys are smitten with her as well, but worrying about her falling into the ocean has been stressful at the very least. Thank goodness for the crew taking turns with her, and for Karol, whom I've started calling 'the puppy whisperer.'

Now that my hands are free, I turn to look back at the yacht, getting smaller in the distance, and then toward the island, which is obviously getting closer. It's been so long—a little more than a month, according to the calendar I made—since I've been on land. I wonder if it will feel funny to walk. Such a thing never would have crossed my mind, not having spent much time on boats, but Karol told me I should expect to feel like I'm still on the yacht, and that there may be a funny swaying sensation in my legs.

I don't mind. I'm just happy at the chance to be on land again, even if it's just for dinner in a restaurant. It will be a nice break, and if all goes according to plan, there may be an opportunity to get myself out of the clutches of the guys. They have no idea I'm thinking this, though, and are under the impression I'm pleased as punch to go out for a spontaneous meal. At least that's what I hope.

Not that it's been horrible to be with them. They've treated me well, dare I say even tried to spoil me. They've given me nice things, treated me respectfully, and well, the sex is freaking off the charts.

It's probably no accident that the guys are taking me ashore after all this time. I've been a good little prisoner, made no trouble for them except for when I tried to take off that one time, and I even pitch in around the yacht to keep myself busy. They seem to like and trust me, as do the crew.

Which is exactly my plan.

The more they trust me, the less they'll be watching over me.

I know they think I have nowhere to go on the island—no money, no passport, no Spanish language skills. And all that is correct. But it's not enough to scare me into submission. There are people on the island who will help me. I have to believe that.

Like the police.

I consider, if I can indeed sneak away, returning to the Airbnb I was supposed to stay in with the French sisters. Will they have my passport and things?

Or will the girls have gotten rid of it all?

I have to try.

My father will be so impressed by my resourcefulness. He'll be proud I got myself out of a difficult, if not impossible, situation. He was hesitant about my going to Europe to begin with, and now that the worst has happened, he'll probably never let me out of his sight again. But if I do get out of this mess, he'll see I can take care of myself. Maybe I'll even get home in time for my actual birthday. Twenty-one is a big deal.

I'd be lying if I didn't say I really, really want to know what Dad did to catch the ire of these guys, and why it's taking so long to rectify it. I'm thinking it must be pretty bad, because I have no doubt he'd move heaven and earth to get me home safely. He's a good man at heart, and while he's an aggressive businessman, I know there's nothing more important to him than *me*, his only daughter. His only remaining family.

When I am freed, Dad will want to punish these men. I know he will. He puts up with no one's shit. The last person who crossed him, Dad bought his business, fired everyone, sold off the assets, and shut it down. He even made money from it in the end. I'm not saying being vengeful like that is how I'd operate, but that's my dad.

After the tender is secured to the dock, we walk a few blocks from the marina to a charming little restaurant, one I vaguely remember seeing on the way in from the airport all those weeks ago when I arrived. At the time, I thought how nice it would be to dine there, and I would have if not for the stupid nightclub. So here I am, finally.

The four of us and the puppy settle in and have a lovely dinner with lots of seafood and wine. The guys are adventurous eaters and have flawless manners. And the fact that the restaurant let me bring the dog is mind-blowing. Europeans are so much more permissive about small pets—they let me keep the puppy on my lap, where she snoozed after I gave her a couple bites of my dinner. Who knew she'd like octopus. But then the guys tell me dogs aren't too picky and eat just about anything you put in front of them.

After dinner, we stroll along the busy Ibiza sidewalks, window shopping and enjoying the scenery. For the first time, I realize I fit in with this beautiful-people crowd, what with my suntan and expensive clothes. It's strange. I never fit in anywhere, and for this to be the place where I finally do is… unexpected. And bizarre. I'm not sure I like it, but it is what it is. I guess spending a month on a yacht will do that for you.

I feel like Julia Roberts in *Pretty Woman*.

And I hate that movie.

Fedor asks us to wait, and he ducks into a

jewelry shop where I'm staring at their window display. I don't wear jewelry aside from my hoops, but this place has some incredible stuff. Not that I could ever afford it. But five minutes later, Fedor emerges with a gold bracelet, which he clasps onto my wrist. It glitters in the last of the day's sun and I have to admit, it is so pretty against my suntan.

"Happy birthday, *krasotka*," he says.

My birthday. How do they know?

"Thank you. It's… amazing. So generous."

I'm sure it's expensive, and now I'm embarrassed. But it's probably just a drop in the bucket for these guys. Wonder if they get jewelry for all the women they kidnap.

They watch me bounce it around on my wrist, admiring it. I do love it. And my birthday is coming up. Weird that they know that.

Actually, no it's not. They know everything.

It's funny, walking around with the puppy on a leash, surrounded by the three guys with Karol watching out for us not far behind. People probably think I'm some rich man's pampered wife. In my floaty white linen sundress and strappy handmade sandals, I look the part. I have a rhinestone headband holding my wild hair off my face, and not a trace of makeup except for red lips. If only I wasn't a prisoner, life would be perfect.

Looking behind us, I pretend to be waiting for Karol to catch up. But I'm really trying to get a good look at a tall thin man in jeans and a dark shirt who seems to be following us. Which I doubt because he really does stick out like a sore thumb and in fact has been easy to spot everywhere we've gone, since the moment we got off the tender.

I don't say anything, but I wonder if the guys or Karol have noticed him. I also wonder if he's someone my father sent to rescue me.

Pausing to look at pretty stationary in a store window, I hope to give the man time to catch up. And while he does get closer, I make eye contact with him before one of the guys puts his hand on my waist to move me along. I want him to know I've noticed him.

He *must* be here for me. If he were an enemy of the guys, I am sure Karol would have dealt with him by now.

After all, I did overhear them talking about bringing firearms for tonight's excursion, so I know someone has a gun. I don't know who, and pretty much don't want to know, but I think if there's an issue the guys can take care of it.

This is my new reality, and it's goddamn crazy, thinking about guns and assessing threats. Just a few weeks ago I was a sloppy tomboy thinking about the upcoming semester at college, and whether Econ would be as hard this year as it was last.

I'm convinced Dad sent someone for me. I know it and I'm thrilled. I'm jumping the gun in this assumption, but I can't imagine any other reason someone would be following us. My father is well-off and knows a lot of people. This is exactly the kind of thing he'd do.

I fake-accidentally drop the puppy's leash and when she starts to dart away, amused pedestrians side-step her, and she runs as fast as her pudgy little legs will carry her. Lucky for me, she heads right in the direction of the mystery man.

A passerby grabs her leash off the ground and with a smile hands it to me. The puppy stops short and turns to see who has the audacity to curtail her exploring and throws a little bark in my direction.

I run to scoop her up in my arms, and then I see the man may not be who I hope he is. Hairs rise on the back of my neck, I'm frozen in place, and my stomach suddenly doesn't feel so great, the wine and seafood I consumed at dinner becoming a noxious mix.

He gives himself away by turning, only for a split second, to look at oncoming traffic, thus revealing his large neck tattoo.

Just like the one I overheard the guys saying local criminals wear. Would this be who my dad sent?

I don't know which way to turn, not that I can move anyway, and for a second I can't breathe. Bogdan jogs to my side and puts his arm around my shoulder, trying to snap me out of my panic.

"Th... th... that man," I whisper, my head down as if I could hide. "Wh... who is he?" I sputter.

"C'mon," Bogdan says. "We have been watching him, baby. Do not worry. Karol has someone on his tail. He is surrounded and doesn't even know it, just another stupid amateur. Dangerous, but still an amateur."

Holy shit. And I thought this man appeared on the scene to rescue me. And that the guys wouldn't have noticed him?

Fuck, am I stupid.

We're walking quickly along the promenade when Bogdan yanks me into an alley. He pushes me behind him and pulls a gun from the back of his pants. He peers around the corner and nods at someone.

"That dirtbag's going to be sorry he got out of bed this morning," he hisses. "Following us. Fucking idiot has no idea what's coming for him."

Karol sticks his head down the alley. "We got

him, Bogdan. The security team has taken him away."

Security team? What security team?

Bogdan looks in every direction around us, sighs, and tucks his gun back into his pants.

"Wh.. what is going on?" I ask in a shaking voice as Fedor and Ilya join us.

Fedor raises an eyebrow at me. "Why don't you tell us, *zolotse?*"

I look from one of them to the other, including Karol. "What? Me? How would I know what's going on?"

Fedor puts his hand on my shoulder. "Let's go. It is not safe out in the open like this."

They just stare, confusing me. Then a large, black SUV pulls up to the curb, and with Fedor in the lead, looking in every direction with narrowed eyes, he gets in and everyone follows, the guys putting me between Bogdan and Ilya in the backseat.

"Wh... where are we going? What's happening?" I ask, nuzzling my chin against the puppy's head.

The driver pushes the car into *drive*, and we peel away from the curb with a screech, momentarily attracting the attention of happy tourists. We take the first left and head uphill, away from the water.

Why are we driving away from the marina? Shouldn't we return to the boat?

In the front seat, Fedor pinches the bridge of his nose with his fingers, like he's fighting a headache. On my left, Ilya takes my hand, and on my right, Bogdan kisses my temple, then looks away, out the window as the SUV gains in elevation.

We pass a few modest houses that get larger the higher we climb, and more spaced apart, as if the closer you are to the top, the more land and home you get. Which I suppose is probably the case.

I don't understand what's happening and I am scared. I wish we were back on the boat, as confining as it is, where I can drop back into my boring but predictable and safe routine.

And still, no one in the car speaks.

"I have no idea who that man was. Do you?" I ask, wishing someone would say something. "Where are we going?"

Maybe someone will at least tell me that.

Fedor finally turns to me. "We are not going back to the yacht, Abby. We are heading to our villa up in the hills."

What?

"I... I don't understand. What villa? How?" I stammer.

My pretty, new bracelet is cold against my wrist, and in the dim light of the SUV, looks like any other old hunk of metal, as if it's been tarnished like my mood and the scary evening. The only thing around me unsullied is the puppy, squirming on my lap to find the perfect snoozing position.

Fedor stares straight ahead. Or is he scanning the horizon? "We have a villa up in the hills," he says. "We will stay there from now on. Karol is making sure all our things from the boat are delivered in the next couple hours. It is safer here."

I don't know how it's safer, but I guess in a boat you're not much more than a sitting duck if someone really wants to get to you.

Disappointment wells up in me, ugly and heavy, pushing me back to the place I was when I first realized I was a prisoner. My hopes about getting away are crushed, obliterated, and now seem so silly and naive. Not only is no one coming to rescue me, we are heading someplace new, someplace I know nothing about, which I doubt will truly be safer.

I stealthily look around at the guys, who are, admittedly, kind to me, but who are also really not the sort of people I want to be with, much less even be aware exist on earth right next to me. I have a lot to learn about being street smart, but some of the things I've seen in the last four-plus weeks have changed me. I'm a different person now and not necessarily for the better. Any innocence I ever had? Gone. Snuffed out.

I'm trying not to feel brittle and dried out inside, but I'm not sure it's working.

The puppy snorts in my arms and I hold her tighter. She and I will be making a trip *somewhere*, god willing, sooner rather than later.

CHAPTER TWELVE

FEDOR

"I DON'T KNOW why my dad hasn't come to get me yet."

Goddamn. The woman has no clue. Absolutely no idea her old man couldn't give a shit about her.

We walk into the villa and I watch for Abby's reaction. Unsurprisingly, her eyes widen and she stops talking.

Yeah, it's that incredible.

And it feels damn good to be off the yacht. Not that I'm complaining. It's just that I was getting a little stir crazy, and am psyched to be in a place now where I can spread out, have some privacy, and enjoy new scenery.

And the scenery is breathtaking. Like more incredible than I even remembered.

The house is massive, all white stucco, with an infinity pool out back overlooking the hills and the ocean beyond. It is decorated in a cool Mediterranean-slash-Moroccan vibe that the last owners must have spent a shitload of money on.

But the house is ours now. Its former owner, a fool of epic proportions, lost it in some sort of business deal. I don't remember the details. It's just one of those 'another day in the office' sort of things. I can't keep track of all our conquests.

But I did hear that shortly after losing the villa, his wife ditched his ass. Poor bastard.

I wander out back on the pretense of checking the water temperature in the pool. I bend to drag my fingers through it and take a deep breath. I've never felt this sort of foreboding about my job before, but we are about to have a conversation with Abby that will most likely leave her devastated.

I don't usually care about shit like this. I mean, business is business. But it's become kind of personal with Abby, given her fucked-up family and, well, the attraction I have to her. Actually, that all of us have to her.

I know she probably hates my fucking guts. I mean, why wouldn't she? Sure, she fucks us, and is pleasant enough, but who wants to be held captive? To have their most important freedoms taken away?

I wouldn't, that's for damn sure.

We never thought we'd be keeping her for so long. We never thought her father would be such a fucker, although in hindsight, his business dealings should have tipped us off. And now, rather than keeping her to use as leverage, we're keeping her to simply save her life.

I'm a vengeful fucker, and I will not let Abby's father get away with what he's doing.

"Fedor, come on in. Let's have a scotch," Bogdan calls.

I know this is hard on him too. He carries his own impossible grief, and I know our current situation dredges all that up again.

In the villa's living room, Abby has crammed herself into a corner of the sofa as the puppy runs around, sniffing her new surroundings. When she loses interest, she scrambles back up on the sofa with Abby's help and curls up next to her.

"Abby," Bogdan starts, "we have some information to share with you."

Hope flashes over her face, as I knew it would. She's wanting good news.

But we're about to douse her optimism.

"I'm going to get right to the point, Abby. The man following us after dinner was not looking to save you."

Her eyes flash with anger. "How do you know?"

We look away from her, knowing our next words are going to change her life.

I wish I could put the moment on hold. Postpone the inevitable. Let this sweet woman believe for a little bit longer that the world is good and kind.

But I can't.

Bogdan gets straight to the point. "Abby, he *was* sent by your father. You're right about that. But he wasn't here to save you. He was here to kill you."

The color drains from her face and her hand covers her mouth.

Yeah, it's like that.

I look away. I have to. The woman deserves some privacy in her moment of agony.

"Wh... what?" she asks, her voice trembling. She continues like she hasn't heard Bogdan. "My father is saving me. He's coming for me. I know he is. You don't know him. You don't know anything. And stop talking about my father that way."

Bogdan looks over at me, and nods in encouragement.

"Abby," I say, taking over, "after we met with your father in Miami, we did some… research. You know, gathered more information on him and… your family."

"You did? What for?"

"Abby, why do you think you father would try to kill you?" I ask.

She looks at each of us, one at a time, like we might tell her we're just making this shit up, that it's a joke, and that everything will be fine.

Afraid not.

"Stop saying that about him—"

"Abby, what happens when you turn twenty-one?" I ask.

Her head whips in my direction and she narrows her eyes. "Why? Why do you need to know that?"

"We already know. We all do. You inherit a shit-ton of money left to you by your mother," Bogdan adds.

She squeezes her eyes shut, like that will make everything go away. If I could make that happen, I would.

"H… how do you know that? Are you trying to steal my money? So you can take everything from

MIKA LANE

me? Why don't you just kill me and throw me on the side of the road? Get it over with," she cries.

Fuck. I knew this would be hard.

"Abby, we don't want your inheritance. Your father does," Ilya says.

She shakes her head and brings her hands to her face. "No. No, he does no. That's a lie."

"Why do you think your mom took off but left you all that money?" I ask.

She takes her hands off her face, red and streaked with tears.

"She left you that money so you could get away from your father just like she had to. She didn't leave because she wanted to. She *had* to."

"I... I don't understand. Dad always said she just up and left. Didn't want to be a wife and mother any longer. Was done with the two of us."

I can't stand the pain in her eyes. She woke up this morning, took a swim in the beautiful Mediterranean Sea, relaxed on the yacht in the sun, then came ashore with us guys for an incredible dinner.

And look at her now. Destroyed. Just destroyed.

"I'm sorry, Abby. Sorry to be telling you this. But you have to know this if you want to remain safe. We're pretty sure your dad is not negotiating with us because if you're... out of the way, he gets

154

your money," I say. "He... he wants us to kill you and if we don't, he will."

The look on someone's face when they realize the life they thought they had no longer exists is one of the most painful things to see.

And that's what I'm looking at right now. I want to comfort Abby, but I doubt she'll let me. She's going to be angry. She's going to rage. And she will take it out on the people in closest proximity—us. That's why we brought her to the villa— she'll be safer here, sure, but she'll also have more privacy for feeling like shit.

As she should.

From across the room, I can feel her sadness. It's unmistakable. And heartbreaking. I almost just want to let her go, walk away, be free. But her life's in danger now, and who knows how long she'll last out there without us guys.

Actually, I know the answer to that. Not fucking long at all. If her dad had the balls to send someone when he knows she's surrounded by us guys, he's pretty fucking desperate for her money. She'd be easy pickings on her own.

I can't have that.

"Karol!" Bogdan calls.

He appears silently, like he always does. I know Karol's been with Bogdan for a long time, but he occasionally gives me the creeps. I keep that to myself, though. The man does a lot of shit for us.

"Yes, boss," Karol answers.

"Is everything all set up in Abby's room? Have her things from the boat been brought?"

He nods almost like a bow. He's strangely formal that way.

"Yes, Bogdan, Miss Abby's room is ready. And I have to say, it's very nice. I think she'll be very comfortable."

We all stand when Abby does, and watch her numbingly follow Karol out of the room.

"We'll need to lock her in. For her own safety," Fedor says.

We nod in agreement.

"Well, that was fucking brutal," I say. "I suggest we take turns checking up on her."

Bogdan rises and pours himself another scotch. He gazes out the window toward the sea, which is getting choppy.

Daylight is mostly gone, and the lack of stars indicates it's overcast. The mounting wind suggests a storm is coming. Perfect for the mood permeating the house.

"I'm glad we've gotten to the bottom of why that bastard isn't responding to our demands. Who would have thought *he* was setting *us* up to

kill his daughter? What kind of father does that?"
I ask.

"Let's make sure Abby's asleep. Then we'll call him."

We reconvene a few minutes later in the living room. I check on Abby, who's nearly catatonic, and give her a light sleeping pill to help her further relax.

We make our call to Miami.

"Hello," Abby's father booms with fake-ass friendliness. "If it isn't my Russian friends."

"Madden, hello. We had an interesting experience tonight," Bogdan says.

Silence.

"It looks like there was a hitman after your daughter. Don't worry, though, we saved her. The guy is probably at the bottom of the ocean by now, tied to a concrete block or something."

Madden clears his throat. "What do you want from me, gentlemen?"

Christ. The fuckery just doesn't stop.

"You know what we want. And we know why you're not delivering," Bogdan says patiently.

Madden laughs. "Okay. If you're so smart, then why don't you tell me?"

God I wish I could reach through the phone and strangle this man.

"You're trying to either get your daughter murdered by us, or have your daughter murdered by someone you hire. We're pretty sure either one works for you, just as long as the job gets done," Fedor says, his voice tight.

Yeah, he is pissed. We all are.

I get closer to the speaker. I want to make sure the fucker hears everything I have to say. "That's why you sent her to Europe this summer, Madden. Here she thinks you've set her up on this great trip for her twenty-first birthday, when you were really setting her up to be killed. What kind of father does that?" I ask.

Madden laughs. "And you think you're so much better? You're the criminals, not me. Look, the longer you guys keep her, the sooner I can have her declared dead. Do what you want with her. You won't see any interference from me. From here on out, she's yours. All yours. I'll just say she got into some trouble on vacation, trusted the wrong people, and *poof!* disappeared. Happens to naïve young women traveling abroad all the time."

There's no getting through to this evil dirtbag.

"So that's it, Madden? You're done with your own daughter? Your own flesh and blood?"

The next thing he says causes a rage in me so great I can't see straight, and at that moment, I know I'll get vengeance on this man if it's the last thing I do.

"Sure guys. Have fun with her. She's yours now. Unless I get to her first."

And the line goes dead.

CHAPTER THIRTEEN

ABBY

IT'S BIZARRE, waking up in the morning in a wonderland like mine, a canopy bed surrounded by floaty white fabric, to look out the huge windows opposite my bed and see the ocean, blue sky, and green hills. Snuggled up next to me is my little puppy, as-yet unnamed, and on my night-stand is a glass of orange juice and a delicious-looking pastry. A soft cotton robe is laid at the foot of my bed, and fuzzy slippers are on the floor just next to it. Fresh flowers fill the vase on my dresser, and my clothes from the day before are folded neatly on the bench outside my closet.

Anyone else would feel like a princess in such

surroundings. And I do, at least for the first few seconds of wakefulness.

Then I remember who I am, and why I'm here. And my wonderland mutates from a dream come true to a weird kind of nightmare. One that I don't quite know what to make of.

I haven't gotten out of bed in two days. The guys have stopped by to distract, console, and entertain me. But I have nothing to say to them. All I can do is turn over on my side in the bed, facing away, and wait for them to give up and leave.

They probably resent me now. Can't wait to be rid of me since I no longer serve them any purpose. Begrudge that I'm taking up space in their house, eating their food, and bringing danger under their roof.

I can't blame them. I feel like a cancer myself. Someone no one wants, and in fact, someone everyone wants to get rid of.

The puppy stirs and I take her over to her pee pad. It's time to start training her, but I haven't had the energy. Which is not fair to her.

Today is the day I will get out of bed, leave my room, and take her for a proper walk to begin her training.

I pull on shorts and a T-shirt, my sneakers, and

a cap. These things and more, all provided by the guys, were brought over from the boat.

One day we're living there, and then we're not. We move to a villa, just like that. No heads up, no discussion, no vote. I am brought here without explanation.

But what do I expect? I am a prisoner, after all.

And now, apparently, a hunted woman.

My sneakers are quiet on the terra cotta tile floors, and I marvel over the villa's boho chic décor, obviously created by someone other than the guys. Most likely a very expensive interior designer. I mean, shit, it's not likely there are a lot of furniture stores on the island. Most everything would have been brought in from elsewhere.

I pad noiselessly through the silent house but don't see a soul. There must be someone around because the food and laundry in my room didn't walk in there by itself.

Holding the puppy and her leash, I stick my head into every room. I look out the glass windows lining the back of the house and see the pool's empty. As I get closer to the kitchen, I finally hear a voice. A male voice. Speaking in a foreign language. It's not quite like the Russian the guys occasionally break into. It's different, somehow, and when I stop outside the kitchen, I realize it's

Karol speaking, I guess in his native Polish. But what's different about his voice is how loud and aggressive it is. He's actually shouting.

He's usually so soft-spoken, and actually sort of passive, at least when speaking to the guys and me. In fact, his subservient manner has made me uncomfortable on many an occasion. Which is why he sounds so strange now.

I find him on the phone, looking out the window, enjoying the same scenery I just woke up to. He has no idea I'm here until the puppy squeaks.

He stiffens when he sees me, ends his call, and gives me his usual broad smile. "Miss Abby," he says, with a bow of his head, "it is good to see you up and about. I hope you are feeling better?"

"I'm fine, thanks, Karol. But what about you? You... sound upset. Why were you yelling?"

He swoops my way and offers me a glass of ice tea, the 'American concoction' of which he is so proud. "I am so sorry to disturb you, Miss Abby. I was... discussing that I needed more help with the villa. It is so large, and we don't have enough staff."

Well, that makes sense. I bet in order to expand his team, he has to make the case to someone, whoever that might be.

"Are the guys not letting you bring on the staff

you need, Karol?" I ask, momentarily forgetting my own shitshow of a life.

He pats me on the back, still smiling broadly. His control is remarkable. "Do not worry about me, Miss Abby."

I set the puppy down and she runs off to sniff every nook and cranny of the kitchen. "You know, Karol, I have nothing to do. Why don't you put me to work?"

I can't believe I'm signing up for housework. A person has got to be seriously fucking bored to do that.

But instead of politely declining my offer, Karol rolls his eyes, scoffs, and exits the kitchen, the sound of his clicking heels fading as he gets further away. Damn. Never seen him act like that before. He's usually all but licking our boots.

There's definitely something up his behind.

I am alone, for the first time in weeks. Really, truly alone in the quiet, beautiful house. At least it seems that way. For the first time since I've been under the guys' control, there is no one watching me. And I am not going to waste this opportunity. But first, I need money. It's bad enough I have no ID or phone.

I poke my head into the hallway and make my way back to the bedrooms. I duck inside the first one I happen upon, belonging to which guy, I don't know, and pull open a couple dresser drawers until I find a small bit of cash. I would prefer to have more, but I stuff the euros in my shorts pocket and head for the door. It's something, at least.

It's strange to be scrounging for money. While my dad isn't rich by any stretch, I've always had everything I needed and most everything I wanted. Not that I wanted much. I've never really been into clothes and things like that. The only reason I'm dressing nicely now is that the guys—or someone they've hired—has shopped for me.

Guess they don't like their prisoners wearing rags.

Maybe this is all a trap. Why is no one breathing down my neck? What suddenly changed? Do the guys no longer care about me since they can't use me as leverage to get my dad to do what they want? How is it they were so vigilant about watching me for the last few weeks and, now that we're back on land, I'm free to do what I want? It makes no sense.

But I'm not wasting this opportunity. The guys might be convinced my father is out to get me, but I can't exactly trust them either, can I?

I step outside the front door waiting for alarms to start blaring, or security guys with big guns to jump out of the bushes. But neither happens. This is actually scarier than if there *were* someone to drag me back into the house and lock me up. Who would have thought a taste of freedom would be so terrifying?

I pull the door closed behind me and follow the first path I see, which twists around a corner and disappears into brushy overgrowth.

The landscape is dry, beautiful in an arid sort of way, with bright pink bougainvillea going crazy here and there. I can't tell if all this grows naturally or is the handiwork of a talented landscaper able to make everything look casually thrown together. It's so different from Miami, all lush and green where gardeners are constantly mowing lawns and trimming hedges.

I pick up my pace almost to a jog, which is the best I can do carrying the puppy. I have no idea where I'm going except downhill, which I figure will eventually lead to something, if not town then at least another house or someplace where I can ask for help. A plane buzzes by overhead, probably heading for the island's airport. It's funny. People come from near and far to visit Ibiza and god knows they spend all kinds of money on their trips here, and yet I am trying desperately to leave.

They'll give anything to get here, and I'm on a mission to escape.

I remain quiet on the path, cradling the puppy and hoping she doesn't suddenly start making noise. Another plane flies overhead and I wonder how the hell I'll ever get on one with no ID. But I'll cross that bridge when I get to it. First things first.

I see the town not far away and without even thinking about it, my pace quickens. I'm free. Finally free. My weeks of captivity are about to be over. And the crazy, sick thing is, I am actually a little sad.

What the fuck, Abby?

I just can't with this. My head is a mess. The guys obviously did a number on me. I guess that Stockholm syndrome shit is really a thing.

But I can't deny, I feel safe with them. The way they protected me that night after dinner was epic. Like I was someone important. Not little old Abby Madden, college student from Miami on her first sojourn to Europe who wears ripped jeans and Converse Chucks.

But I can't live locked up. That's bullshit. No one wants that.

And yet.

Am I running just because the opportunity presented itself? Is this really the solution to the problem? Escaping has been on my mind for so long that my action today is just the default. I saw an open door, and I ran through it, literally and figuratively.

I'm breathing hard from my light jog, clearly out of shape from sitting around on my ass on that yacht for weeks. But I see a crossing guard and dodge traffic to get to her.

Donde ésta la policía?

That's about all I remember from my high school Spanish, and I am hoping against hope the guard understands my hideous pronunciation.

She looks at me, surprised I've accosted her in the middle of a busy street, and points. "*Señorita,* it is that way," she says, gesturing with her chin.

She speaks English!

Ohthankgod.

She kindly stops traffic so I can get back to the curb alive, shaking her head at another careless, idiotic tourist. I follow the signs for *policía* and after a couple blocks find it right off the main drag.

I run inside and am not sure whether to laugh or cry.

I'm here. I'm saved. Oh my god. I can go home. Or somewhere.

"*Habla inglés, Señor?*" I ask.

I'm embarrassed by my Spanish, but I figure

they hear dummies like me all the time butchering their language.

The bored cop behind the thick, bulletproof glass nods. Guess they don't see much crime in a beautiful place like Ibiza.

Wait till he hears my story.

"I've been kidnapped. I need help," I blurt, knowing I sound like a crazy woman.

But I don't care. *I'm free.*

And while the hairs on the back of my neck bristle as I wonder why this is so damn easy, I shove the feeling aside. I need to focus. I need to call my father and find out what the hell is going on.

"Excuse me, *Señorita?*"

"I... I... I have been kidnapped. I just escaped. I need to call my father back in the United States. Please help me."

He looks around and slowly gets up from his stool. He opens the locked door to the waiting room and beckons me inside. It securely clicks behind us.

"Thank you, sir. Thank you so much. I've been a prisoner for weeks. I just need to call my father at home in the United States."

He ushers me into a small room with a table and a couple chairs, like the ones you see on TV. I think they're called interrogation rooms or something.

"Sir, do you think I could use the phone first? I really need to call home.

He gestures for me to take a seat. "In a moment, *Señorita*. Let me get you some water first."

I set the puppy down and she crazily runs around, sniffing everything in the room.

"Oh, thank you. Yes, I could use some water."

He pulls the door closed behind me and I want to jump up and down. I don't believe what the guys told me about my father. They're full of shit. They know nothing about my dad or me. He'll be thrilled to know I'm safe now.

I can't wait to get off this fucking island. I will never come back to Spain. Never.

I sit in the room for several minutes, drumming my fingers. There is absolutely nothing to do but wait, so I play with the puppy a bit, not even caring when she pees on the floor.

I don't understand what is taking so long, so I check the door, which is indeed locked. Fine. That's probably how it's supposed to be. So I knock.

No answer.

I knock again. "Hello!" I shout.

And finally, footsteps click down the hallway toward me. I sigh with relief.

The door flies open and the cop hands me my water.

And just behind him are Bogdan, Fedor, and Ilya.

CHAPTER FOURTEEN

BOGDAN

"Do you have everyone in your fucking pocket?"

Abby is not happy.

In the SUV, Karol steers around the last, steep switchback, and we arrive at the villa. Fedor has the puppy, and I release the zip-ties from Abby's hands.

When Karol notified us that Abby was missing, there was a pit the size of a bowling ball in my stomach. Shocked the shit out of me. I didn't expect to feel that way.

She's a prisoner, not a relative. Not a girlfriend. Not even a colleague.

We kidnapped her to force her father's hand.

And now that's all cocked up because he wants her dead.

I grip Abby's wrist as I direct her inside the house. Her eyes are dark and hateful, and I wouldn't put it past her to try and slug one of us.

It's funny, but when Karol said she'd taken off, a part of me was insulted. Like, my feelings were hurt. Which is fucking bizarre.

How could I be acting like such a little bitch over someone we have in our possession just to further our own interests? Someone we couldn't give a shit about?

Because I do give a shit about her.

And that's a problem.

In fact, I'm afraid it's been a problem for a while.

And she's pissed off right now, seething and seeing red. Although, I swear to god after the shock of seeing us guys at the police station there to collect her, there was a modicum of relief that washed over her face. Like we cared enough to come pull her out of what could have been a dangerous situation.

Fuck, maybe I'm flattering myself, blinded by her beauty and... everything. But does she really think she can get away from us? The moment she walked into the island's joke of a police station, the guys there knew to call us.

It pays to have friends in low places. It doesn't cost a whole hell of a lot, either. An occasional bottle of scotch, covering a kid's school tuition, or even a trip somewhere for a big favor—like today's —and those guys bend over backward for us.

Abby's resisting my hold, which I suppose is to be expected. She's ambivalent. It's all over her face. On one hand, all she can think is to get the hell out of here. On the other, she knows she has nowhere to go. She might not be ready to completely accept it, but I think deep down she knows what we told her about her dad is true.

I push her into her room, and pull the door closed. But she stops me.

"Bogdan. Let me call my dad. Just let me use your phone and get the answers I need. Please. I promise I won't run again."

Yeah, when pigs fly.

But, what the fuck. Let her find out for herself. It'll hurt—again—but at least she'll get the answers she's so desperate for. It will be to everyone's benefit.

Her hands shake as she dials from my phone. She puts the call on speaker without my having to ask.

It rings several times. It's only six p.m. or so in Miami, so Madden should be around.

"Hello, Stacey? Stacey, it's Abby."

There are several seconds of silence and I wonder if the call's been disconnected.

"Oh. Hello, Abby," an uninterested female voice says.

Abby frowns. "What are you doing with my dad's cell phone, Stacey? Never mind I need to talk to him. It's an emergency. Right now. Please," she begs.

Long sigh. Fuck, if this is her dad's secretary, he needs to get a new one. Unless she's doing exactly what he's asked her to.

Which wouldn't surprise me.

I can see it now, Madden telling the secretary he doesn't want to talk to his daughter. Fucking asshole.

"Hold on," the secretary says in a bothered voice.

The background noise goes silent, indicating she put the phone on mute. Bitch was probably telling Madden right now that his daughter is on the phone, and trying to find a way to get rid of her.

But Abby's face is hopeful. Positive. Maybe

even a little excited. Guess she's misses the old man.

I fucking hate this for her.

I feel protective. Yeah, that's what it is. I feel protective of her. And that hasn't always worked out well for me.

"Hello? Hello, Abby?" the secretary says impatiently.

"Yeah? Where's my dad?"

"Your dad's not available right now."

To say the hope melted off Abby's face is an understatement. It might be more accurate to say the very life melted off her face.

She looks down and passes the phone to me, which I swipe closed.

Taking a seat on the edge of the bed, she absent-mindedly runs her open palms over her thighs.

"Are you cold, Abby?" I ask.

It's not cold. In fact, because it's the middle of the day, it's hot.

She runs her hands up and down her arms and nods.

So, I take a seat next to her and pull her to me, burying my nose in her sweet-smelling hair. She nestles closer to me and sighs.

It's funny. I thought she'd rage when she finally

accepted the truth. Throw stuff. Break things. Scream and shout.

Instead, she's like a balloon that's had ninety percent of its air leaked. That's what it is. She's a shell.

She looks up at me. "Maybe you were right about him."

I run my fingers through her hair. Fuck, I could get used to this. "I'm sorry, *zolotse*. So sorry."

She sighs, still looking up at me, and then leans closer, surprising me with a kiss. I hold her face as she parts her lips, letting me taste her.

I pull back. "I really am sorry, Abby."

She shrugs. "Shit happens, I guess," she says hollowly. "But who would have thought you were a softie? That all you guys are softies?"

She's regarding me with a smirk, and I see some of the life coming back to her face. Along with some uncharacteristic hardness. Uncharacteristic, and most likely permanent.

"Well, keep it a secret, please," I say.

"Or what? You'll kill me?" she laughs.

We never would have killed her. It would have been impossible. Simply impossible. But I don't want to talk about that.

I have more important things on my mind at the moment, not least of which is my raging hard-on. And the scent of Abby's pussy drifting from her loose shorts.

She gets to her feet and starts to undress. I know her well enough now to know she's trying to forget. And I am happy to help.

"Your bedroom door's open," I say.

She glances over her shoulder. "Good."

And as if she'd summoned them, Fedor and Ilya appear, both at the same time.

"Hey, guys, anyone up for a swim in the pool—" Fedor starts to say.

But stops short. For obvious reasons.

Abby is now nude, and she saunters over to the guys, who are enthusiastically eating her alive with their gaze. She takes each by the hand and brings them over to the bed. But not before Fedor kicks the door closed.

I knew I liked that guy.

Fuck, she's sexy. I want to kiss the shit out of her. I want to fuck the shit out of her. I want to make her scream and squirm. I want to make her feel pleasure and pain, separately, and together.

I'm whipped. That's all there is to it.

Fedor makes the first move, the fucker. Can't blame him. If I'd moved faster, I'd be the cock-blocker.

"*Malishka*, lie down and spread yourself," he says.

Her pupils dilate and she smiles slightly. She inches back on the bed, propped up by her elbows, and bends her knees. Then she slowly pulls them opens partway.

"Keep going," he says, waving his hand in demonstration.

She huffs and opens them more.

"Do I have to open them for you, *malishka*?" he asks, moving toward her. "Or do you think you can do it yourself?"

She rolls her eyes and shrugs, then looks off in the distance, out the window at the ocean.

Fedor pulls down his shorts and leaps on the bed, pushing Abby's hips open with his body. He grabs her two hands and extends them over her head, holding them there. She is pinned now.

"Guys. Each of you take one leg," he says.

Her eyes widen and worry passes over her face. It doesn't completely go away.

Which makes my dick so hard it hurts.

Yeah, honey, you are about to get something you'll never forget.

Ilya and I position ourselves on either side of her, each pushing one of her knees back nearly to her shoulders. Then, Fedor slams into her. She squirms under him, unable to move anything more than her head, which he grabs with his free hand by taking a fistful of her hair and pulling it. Her neck bends at what is most certainly an uncomfortable angle, but she continues to wear a spaced-out smile and is moaning lightly. It's a beautiful fucking sight.

Grinning, Fedor pushes Ilya and me away and flips over, pulling Abby on top of him. He holds her to his chest and bucks his hips as he continues to fuck her. This gives us a beautiful view of her juicy pussy and rosebud ass, and I pull my dick out of my pants because there is just no more waiting. I crawl up on the bed behind her and dribble some spit down the crack of her ass. I massage her bottom briefly to let her know what's coming, and then press into her. I have no doubt this is her first double penetration.

Fedor stills so I can get inside and when I do, her head drops with a groan. She holds him with one hand, her nails digging into his arm, and reaches behind her to keep me from being too aggressive.

Can't say I blame her.

I gradually slide further inside, and Fedor and I take turns pumping her. The three of us are moving in unison and the room is full of grunting and groaning. I know my orgasm is near and I have no intention of drawing it out—I don't want to leave our beautiful girl too sore.

But when Ilya positions himself at her side and puts her hand on his cock. The image of her being fucked by all three of us is seared into my brain as something I know I'll never forget.

She begins to scream like some sort of feral beast, and I lose my load and my mind at the same time, my vision clouding, and all I can think is she can never leave us.

CHAPTER FIFTEEN

ABBY

"You're fucking kidding me."

I nod in embarrassment at Fedor. Now the guys really know what an idiot I am.

Shaking his head, he laughs. "You've been drinking espresso all this time and you don't even like it?"

Pretty much. I'm just so done with having espresso every morning and after every meal. It's disgusting, bitter sludge and there is no way I will tolerate another sip of it. So, I confess, to the amusement of the guys.

I figure while I'm sharing other shit, I may as well come clean about this.

Yes, I have more than one secret to share.

After screwing up my courage, because it was going to suck balls if it backfired on me, I informed the guys I like them. As in, I am *attached to them, like them*. And now I'm hoping I don't end up regretting showing my hand.

The guys just triple-teamed me. At least I think that's what it's called. And it was heaven, pure heaven. I loved every second of it and want to do it again, soon. It was powerful, beautiful, and fucking hot. It was different from any experience I've ever had.

Or was *I* different?

We're catching our breath now, sprawled on my bed. Somehow, incredibly, I am surrounded by three Greek-god-like men, who are all touching me, holding on to me, like I'm a lifeline.

Works for me. I'll be their lifeline.

But before I get too comfortable, I scoot to the bathroom to clean up. And when I look in the mirror, I don't recognize the woman looking back at me.

My face is different than it was three or four weeks ago. It's different from last night. And it's different from when I'd gotten up that morning. I just don't look like Abby Madden, college student from Miami, anymore. I look relaxed. Worldly.

Well-fucked. Slightly pretty. The same but not the same.

Is what I'm looking at *happiness*? Am I happy? I'm a goddamn prisoner, I just learned some terrible things about my father, and the future I thought I had ahead of me is now pretty well disintegrated.

But strangely, I feel okay. Maybe for the first time in forever.

It's when I'm back in bed that I share my news. They look at me and nod, not saying anything, but I believe I know what they're thinking—that they like me just as I like them. They're just not ready to say it.

And if I'm wrong?

Fuck 'em. Their loss.

Although, now that they can't send me back to my father, I don't know what the hell they think they're going to do with me. I mean, I'm pretty much their problem now. And they're not about to throw me out on the street, I'm sure of that.

A couple more peaceful weeks pass incredibly quickly, and my attempted escape seems to be forgotten. Old news. At the time, they didn't seem happy about. Maybe it was an act, to scare me into submission. But now it's like it never happened.

The best news is, that since we're at the villa, I

have a lot more to do to fill my days, the least of which is training the puppy. It takes up a bunch of my time although I have to admit it's great fun. I can see that for the person who's working full-time and has a hundred other things to do, dealing with a puppy is stressful. But since I have all the time in the world, the puppy and I can move gradually.

And I've named her. Finally.

She's called Bonita, since I came by her in Spain, and it looks like she's already answering to it. At a little over three months of age, she seems to have mastered sit, stay, and down. Come and heel are coming a bit more slowly, but that's ok because we're having a blast. I adore my pudgy little tank, and after she eats, you should see how full her belly is.

I can't imagine my life without her.

The guys love her too and I can tell they're a little jealous when she goes to one of them and not the other.

The only one she doesn't like is Karol, which cracks us up. The quietest, most gentle person in our group is the very one she avoids, actually hiding when he enters the room. But I am sure that, in time, she'll warm up to him.

Another good thing about being off the boat

and here on the island is going to restaurants. Not that the food on the boat wasn't great—it was. It's just that getting dressed up and going out is so much fun, as is the variety of food.

Except the place we went to tonight.

I've taken to ordering octopus almost everywhere I go. First, I love it, and second, every restaurant makes it a little differently. It's some sort of Mediterranean thing.

Unfortunately, tonight, it didn't agree with me. In fact, it was like I'd ingested something old and rotten, which I knew I hadn't, but my digestive system sure was acting like it. Like I'd insulted it with something strange and foreign and that it wanted to get back at me for it.

Thanks, stomach.

So after dinner, I head to my room to ride it out. After opening my window for fresh air and lying down, there's a knock on my door.

"Hello?" I call weakly.

Bogdan pops his head inside. "Can I come in?"

I nod, pushing myself up in bed, and he brings me a tray with chicken broth and tea.

"This is what Russians have when they don't feel well," he says, setting it on my nightstand and taking a seat on the edge of my bed.

The thought of eating again turns my stomach

until I get a whiff of the broth. I nearly knock Bogdan out of the way grabbing for the mug of salty, golden deliciousness. After chugging almost all of it, I lean back onto my headboard, and sigh, my eyes closed.

"Thank you," I whisper, the warm liquid instantly calming me.

"My *babushka* used to make this when someone was sick. I gave Chef the recipe so he could replicate it."

I lick my lips, hoping I don't look like a greedy pig. "That was heavenly. Pure heaven," I breathe as I wave the steaming tea under my nose.

Bogdan pats my head and stands to leave. "Get some rest, *malishka*. I'll check back in a bit."

"Thank you. Love you," I murmured happily.

What?

What the fuck did I just say?

No, no, no, no.

But, bless him, instead of compounding my embarrassment, he winks and pulls the door closed behind him to leave me to doze off, wallowing in my big-mouthed misery.

I vow to eat no more octopus.

The next thing I know, I'm startled awake by another knock on my door. I look around, surprised to find my room dark. I figure I've been out for a few hours.

My stomach feels better, though.

"Come in," I call.

Ilya opens the door, flanked by Bogdan and Fedor. I hope they aren't looking for playtime. I'm not up for that at the moment.

"Hey, guys," I say, trying to perk up my energy while pulling the bedsheets to my chin.

They stand there for a moment until Ilya speaks. "How do you feel about having a visitor?"

Visitor? Who the hell would visit *me*? Maybe my dad? No. No way. The French girls? Fuck them.

I shrug. "I... I guess that would be fine. Who is it?" I ask.

Ilya returns to the hallway and guides a woman through my door and into my room.

She's about my height and has wild black hair like I do. She forces a smile, but her bottom lip is quivering too hard to pull it off.

I know this woman. I haven't seen her in fifteen years, but I'd know her if a hundred years had passed.

What the hell?

It's my mother, Nanette Madden.

At least, I think it's my mother. Could this be a joke? Did they find someone who looks like my mom, just fifteen years older than the last time I saw her?

Would someone really do that?

"Abby," she says cautiously, her voice breaking.

My mouth is so dry I can't speak. Not that I'd know what to say, in any case. But this is my mother. It's no imposter. I know my own mother.

But what the fuck?

I look at the guys, their expressions giving away nothing.

"When we were doing a background check on your father, we found your mother, as you can see," Ilya explains. "Living in Paris."

I open my mouth to speak but just snap it shut again. Words aren't working for me at the moment.

"Honey, I have so much to tell you," she says, moving toward the bed.

But I put out a hand to stop her.

I'm thoroughly confused by the myriad thoughts tumbling around my head, but two things are clear.

Why has she come?

And why should I give a shit?

After all, she bailed on Dad and me a long time ago. And what with my recent discovery about Dad, I am starting to get used to the idea that I have no parents. None at all. Betrayed by both, just in different ways, I'm writing Dad off just like I did Mom a long time ago.

"Wh... what are you doing here?" I finally stumble in a breaking voice.

Her face starts to crumble. "Oh, baby, I've missed you so much. I've dreamt of the day I would see you again."

I frown at her. "If that's the case, then why did you leave?"

Against my protests, she rushes to the bed and kneels down next to it, reaching for my hands, which she desperately clings to. "Oh, honey, he made me leave. Told me if I ever came back, both our lives would be in danger. He's an evil, evil man."

At this point, she hangs her head and quietly cries. But she has a death grip on my hands.

"Who? Who did this? Who sent you away?" I nearly called her *Mom*. Nearly.

"Your father, honey. He's the one who sent me away."

CHAPTER SIXTEEN

ILYA

I'D BE LYING if I didn't admit to having a tear in my eye over the reunion of Abby and her mother. I suppose we should have left the room and given them some privacy, but we weren't at all sure how things were going to go and wanted to be on hand in case the happy reunion went south.

As it is, things are awkward as fuck. No surprise there. What do you say to a mother you haven't seen since you were five years old? What do you say to a daughter you left fifteen-plus years ago? And I thought my family situation was fucked up.

As it turns out, mother and daughter have a lot to say to each other.

"Honey, I know this situation is not ideal, but thank god you're away from your father."

Abby looks at her skeptically, as if she wants to believe. But she has no reason to trust this woman. Yet.

"What do you mean?" Abby asks in a flat voice, as if she's trying to provoke. Can't blame her. I'd be full of anger too.

"Honey, you're nearly twenty-one. You will inherit your trust in a few days. You can't let your father touch it, as much as he would like to. As much as he might pressure you to let him access it. Please don't do it."

Turmoil crosses Abby's pretty face, not helped by the fact that she's still pale from her bout with food poisoning. I make a mental note to ask Chef to put together another tray of chicken broth and tea.

"Why are you here?" she asks her mother, pointblank.

This is where I insert myself into the conversation. "Abby, we found your mom and brought her here. Her story is compelling. You need to hear it."

She looks from me back to her mother. "What story? That you left Dad and me when I was five?"

Nanette stifles a sob. We knew this was not going to be easy, reuniting these two. Talk about dredging up painful shit.

"Abby, I didn't leave voluntarily. Your father sent me away, like I said."

Abby shook her head vehemently. "No. No he didn't. You *left* us," she says, inching away from her mother.

Nanette reaches for her. "Abby, that's not true. That's what he told you. He wanted to get rid of me because I knew too much about his business. Told me if I didn't take off, he'd have me committed and would send you away somewhere. He gave me a large sum of money and sent me on my way. But I put that money aside for you."

"Wh... why?" Abby asks.

Nanette's face is soaked with tears as she appeals to her daughter. "Oh, honey, I knew the time would come when you'd need to get away from him yourself. The money is to help you do that. I had to wait until you were twenty-one for you to access it. Otherwise, I was afraid your father would get his hands on it."

Abby stares at her mom, years of lies and deceptions working to untangle themselves in her mind. It's bad enough she found out her dad's a murderous scumbag who doesn't give a shit about her, but now she finds out he also robbed her of her mother. If she doesn't turn bitter and hard after this, it will be miraculous.

Fuck all. It's early in the day and all I can think is I'd like a scotch.

I want to go to Abby and comfort her, or at least try to. Take away her pain if it's at all possible. Make her forget the shitiness that has been her life in recent days, and give her something to smile about, driven as I am to keep the people close to me safe. And, for better or worse, Abby is close to me. To us. All of us.

Whether she likes it or not.

Her mother makes one last appeal. "I knew you would eventually want to get away from him. That you would learn, in time, what kind of person he really is."

Abby frowns. "But why didn't you just tell me? Why didn't you try to contact me all these years?"

Nanette shakes her head. "I couldn't. Your father always knew where I was, even when I went to France to escape his reach. He still managed to keep tabs on me. I couldn't risk letting him alienate you before you were old enough to leave. I was afraid for you. And for myself."

Abby looks over at us guys. She's suspicious,

still weighing her mother's story. "How... how did you find her?" she asks us, like she needs proof.

Fedor approaches the bed. "It was easy, Abby. We... know a lot of people, and they're quite helpful when we need them. After we found out that your dad was... not the person you thought he was, we tracked your mom down in France to see if she might want to come back into your life."

Nanette nods. "That's right, honey. I jumped at the chance to reconnect with you, for one, but also to protect you. I couldn't help you all these years. He wouldn't let me. But I can now. If you'll let me."

Abby looks down at her hands, and her shoulders start to shake. "I... I don't know how this could happen. Who does shit like this?" she cries. "My... my dad did all this? What's wrong with him? What's wrong with *me*?"

Aw, hell. I hate to see my girl in pain. If only I could carry that for her. I can't see her face, but the tears dropping onto her folded hands tell me all I need to know.

Goddammit.

"Abby, this is what I think we should do," Ilya says, grabbing a seat on the bed and taking her hand. "If you're well enough, let's do a video call with your father. I think that will clear things up for you."

Shit. I don't know if that's a good idea. But maybe cutting to the chase is the best policy. Rip off the bandage, as they say.

She stares back at Ilya and slowly nods. He pulls his phone out of his back pocket and dials Abby's father, then hands her the phone.

While it's ringing, she wipes her tears with the corner of the bed sheet and holds a finger to her lips to silence the four of us. I help Nanette to her feet. She's been kneeling next to Abby's bed for so long her legs must be numb.

"Dad. Hi," she says with a firm voice.

"Abby? Oh my god, it's you," he says, all concerned like the fake-ass bastard he is. "Stacey told me you·called. Whose phone is this? Where are you?"

Abby falters, probably trying to figure out where to start. Perhaps it was too soon to shove a phone in her face. Maybe we should have given her time to collect her thoughts.

But she handles herself like a champ. "Dad, I think you know where I am and who I am with."

Silence.

"How are you?" he asks nervously.

How the fuck does he think she is? He's well aware she was kidnapped because of his actions. And he's acting like nothing is going on?

Fucker.

"I'm okay, I guess. It's pretty here. I have a puppy. I named her Bonita. I've been eating good Spanish food, although last night I had some octopus that didn't sit well…"

Abby continues to babble on with her awkward small talk like nothing is wrong at all, like she hasn't been missing for weeks, her dad responding with an occasional, bland *uh-huh* and *that's nice*. Pretending like everything is normal.

But he doesn't seem too happy his daughter is doing well. No big surprise there.

With no mention of what he might be doing to get her home, he cuts right to the chase. "So honey, now that you're almost twenty-one, you can access the trust left to you by your mother. Shall I call my attorney for you?" he offers.

He must really think his daughter's an idiot. Foolish man.

"Oh, no thanks, Dad. I'll get my own attorney."

He scoffs. "Honey, this is not the sort of thing you have any experience with. I'm happy to help you."

The guys and I look at each other, certain he'd *love* to fucking help. Help empty out her account, that is.

And then she lets him have it.

"Dad, I know you're trying to get your hands on my money—"

"Excuse me," he bellows. "What are you talking about—"

But she cuts him off. That's our girl. "I know about Mom too. I know you've lied to me my whole life. And I have news for you. You will never see me again. And you'll never get your hands on my money."

Madden explodes with such vehemence and rage I can't even make out what he's saying. But I don't need to. He's a narcissist of the first degree, and when people like that don't get their way, they lose their shit.

He's been called out, and he's triggered.

Too fucking bad. If he were here in the room with us... well, things wouldn't end well for him. That's all I can say.

"You little bitch," he screams. "All I've done for you, you spoiled little girl."

"*You,*" she yells, "you can fuck right off! You've manipulated me all these years. Rot in hell, asshole!"

She throws the phone down on the bed and falls into Nanette's arms.

Every ending is a new beginning. And today, Abby's beginning something very important.

ABBY and her mom have a quiet dinner with us, then go to their respective rooms, exhausted by the tumultuous day. This gives the guys and me a chance to talk and to debrief. We head out to sit by the pool. It's a gorgeous night and I tip my head back to watch a shooting star.

"Christ," Fedor says, "not that I'll ever have kids, but if I did, I sure would do better than that dirt-bag, Madden. What a sick fuck."

I had my challenges growing up. We all did. But there's just no excuse for someone like Madden, who's surrounded by privilege. The man can have anything he desires, and he is still a thieving fucker. Nothing will ever be enough for him.

I'd feel sorry for the man if I didn't detest him so much.

Damn, I need to shake this off.

"Hey, anyone want a cigar? I'm going to get one," I say.

Both Fedor and Bogdan nod, and I head into the house.

But before I can get to the humidor, I hear Bonita scratching somewhere in the house. I follow the sound and find she's closed up in the kitchen, which is strange because she usually sleeps in Abby's room. I open the kitchen door for her, and she scoots out, heading straight for Abby. I poke my head around the corner to watch her, when she yelps.

Abby's door is closed and I figure the dog wants in, so I head down the hallway to help. But when I get there, her door is open, and in the dark, I see someone moving. And that someone is not Abby. What the fuck.

I flick on the light.

It's Karol, holding a knife. A big knife.

It takes me a second to react. I am caught so off-guard that I assume I'm seeing things at first. But the adrenaline kicks into high gear, and I lunge.

Karol's not particularly big or strong, so tackling him is easy. I get him on the ground and kick the knife away, all while he's struggling like it will do him some good.

Abby sits up, rubbing her eyes. "What the hell is going on?" she asks, lifting the upset puppy to the bed.

Fedor and Bogdan appear in the door.

"What... what happened?" Fedor asks, looking from the knife, to me on top of Karol, to Abby.

Bogdan crosses the room and pulls Karol to his feet, pulling his arm up behind his back. Karol winces with both pain and annoyance. "Can you explain what you were doing in Abby's room, Karol? With a knife?"

Karol, the mild-mannered staff member who's been with Bogdan all his life, turns to us, baring his teeth. "Did you think I was going to be your slave forever?" he spits. "The girl's father offered to pay me more than you ever would. It was my way out. My way out of this... indentured servitude."

"What?" Bogdan asks quietly. "You're no indentured servant. You could always leave whenever you wanted."

Karol screws up his face, his hatred palpable. "I'm tired of being taken advantage of, waiting on you rich people like you're above me. Madden offered me enough money to make me a rich man. I was going to leave and never be seen again. I'd be a fool to pass that up."

Abby gets out of bed and approaches Karol. But Bogdan is careful to keep him out of her reach. If there is any punishing to do, that's best left to us guys.

"You... you were going to kill me?" Abby asks in a small voice.

Karol narrows his eyes at her. "Don't be so naïve, silly girl. It doesn't suit you."

Bogdan pulls Karol's arm up higher, and he screams from the pain. But it also shuts him up.

"Karol, I don't understand. I thought you were happy working for me. For us," Bogdan says, vacillating between incredulity and anger.

And confusion.

Karol grins wickedly. "You are a bigger fool than I thought. I've detested you and your family for years. I've been looking for a way out, and when I approached Madden, he was all too happy to make a deal with me."

"Oh my god," Abby says, her hand flying to her mouth.

Bogdan is crushed. I don't think I've seen such sadness in his eyes since he lost his sister. I mean, Karol is like family to him. At least that's what we thought all these years.

He looks at Fedor and me. "Can you guys take care of him? I don't think I can do it."

Fedor takes Karol and leads him out of the room. I follow just behind.

We've addressed many a problem like this before by 'taking care' of the matter.

Never thought Karol would be one of those problems, though.

CHAPTER SEVENTEEN

ABBY

I GET to the bathroom just in time to lose everything I had for tonight's dinner.

Karol.

I never would have guessed.

Who would have?

He's the guys' foot soldier. Right hand man. Fixer. There was nothing he couldn't do. Or wouldn't do.

And underneath his supposed happy subservience, he'd been steaming for years? How does someone fake satisfaction for that long? Why did he never say anything? Was he just biding his time for an opportunity like the one he got with my father?

I get sick again.

Bogdan depended on him so much. If he'd only known Karol was unhappy, I'm sure he would have done anything to persuade him he was valued. Instead, the man let his resentment fester and fester, until he couldn't take it anymore and cracked. What a terrible mistake. One he'd pay dearly for, most likely with his life, if I know these guys at all.

I'd overheard him say how grateful he was to Bogdan's family. How they'd gotten him out of Poland, where he was in no end of trouble, gave him a job and fair wage, and got him on the straight and narrow.

Or at least as straight and narrow as you can get working for guys like Bogdan, Fedor, and Ilya.

Bogdan is crushed. Maybe even devastated. Shattered.

I am too.

"Oh, honey," my mother said, joining me in the bathroom and rubbing my back. Just like a real mom. "Bogdan just came and woke me up."

I wanted to cry, but I couldn't. It was like my tears were all dried up.

"How... how could you leave me?" I asked quietly. "I was only five years old."

She paused, then took a deep breath. "It was the hardest thing I've ever done. But I did it because you were the most important thing to me in the world. I chose you. Over myself, over everything else. It was the only way to keep you safe. Your father is vindictive. I was afraid of what he might do to you, to punish me."

"Did you know of his... business dealings? The shady ones?" I ask.

She helps me up off my knees and to the edge of the tub, which is cool against my bare legs. I pull a large bath towel around my shoulders for a little warmth, and shiver.

My mother hangs her head. "Yes. Of course. That's why he used you against me, to keep me quiet. He paid me off and sent me away. But he never imagined I'd save that money for you, so you could escape someday too."

"How did he find out? *When* did he find out?"

She rubbed her temples and shook her head slowly. "He found out sometime in the last couple years. He wasn't supposed to know, but as your twenty-first birthday drew near, the trustee sent something to the house. Your father intercepted it."

She gave me a sad smile, her eyes crinkling in

the corners. It might have been fifteen years since I'd last seen her, but she was still stunning.

"He sent me on this trip to kill me." I shivered and another wave of nausea washed over me.

My mother put an arm around me and pulled me to her. "I wouldn't put it past him, honey."

I hung my head. I had no idea how I would ever recover from this. "I... I feel like my life is over."

"I know. I felt that way once. But I don't anymore," she said, smoothing her fingers through my hair. "We're back together, Abby. Regardless of the circumstances, this is a good thing. I've been dreaming of this day for fifteen years."

There was a knock on the bathroom door.

"Come in," I called.

"Just wanted to check on you two," Bogdan said, peering around the door.

All eyes were on me as I got to my feet. "I'd like to talk to Bogdan. Alone... if you don't mind," I said to my mother.

I wasn't ready to call her *mom* yet.

"Of course. I'll be in the kitchen. I don't think I can sleep now. If you need anything, just holler." She kisses the top of my head. "But you try to get some sleep, okay? I know it won't be easy, but you need it with all you've been through."

"Thank you... Mom."

Holy shit. I said it.

And my words are not lost on her. Her eyes fill with tears as she nods at the two of us and leaves the room.

This leaves me with Bogdan. "Want to go out to the pool?" I ask.

He waves his arm. "After you, *zolotse*."

We pad barefoot over the terra cotta tiles until we reach the pool deck. The evening breeze makes me feel like I can breathe again, and in the far-off distance, moonlight glitters on the ocean, reminding me there are still beautiful things in this world.

"Just breathtaking," I whisper.

It's bizarre, being surrounded by such magnificence, but also a life in such shambles.

"I'm going in for a swim," Bogdan says, pulling his T-shirt off and dropping his shorts and boxers.

Goddamn, he was delicious naked.

I glanced toward the house. "What about my mom?"

He shrugs. "She's in bed. But it's also dark out." He dives in and surfaces at the other end of the pool.

Oh, what the hell.

I shrug off my nightgown and dive right in after him. And I'm so glad I do. The water calms me, momentarily soothing some of the day's rough edges. It doesn't eradicate them altogether, not that I expect it to, but it does provide some relief, and for that I'm grateful.

I swim over to Bogdan, where he's resting on the edge of the infinity pool.

"Such a pretty girl. You look like a mermaid with your hair slicked back and water dripping from your eyelashes."

He leans forward to kiss me deeply, and in spite of all that's been going on, I feel that familiar clench between my legs, like a little friend calling out, 'hey, I'm down here, don't forget about me.'

I almost laugh at that. But I have something serious to talk about.

"I want him punished," I say. "My father."

Holy shit. I said it. I actually said it.

Bogdan looks at me silently.

So I continue. "He's a bad man. If he isn't taken care of, he will never leave me alone."

I wait for him to say something. He's choosing his words carefully, I can tell. He doesn't take what I'm asking for lightly, and I respect that.

"Consider it done," he says simply.

Wow. That's all there is to it? I put in an order, and the guys fill it?

"How will you do it? When will you do it?"
I ask.

Bogdan runs a finger down my chest until he reaches my erect nipple. "Don't worry about that."

"Will you tell me when you've done it?" I ask.

He laughs. "Yes, *malishka*. Yes, I will."

Relief washes over me in a rush so intense, I am scared. Am I that vengeful? Am I that hateful? Have I asked that my own father be killed?

Am I just as bad as he is?

As if he hears my concerns, Bogdan lifts me up onto the edge of the pool, and pushes my legs open, as if he's telling me to stop thinking so hard. And before I know it, he's buried his face between my legs, running his tongue along my wet slit, dipping inside me, flicking around my clit, then fucking me with his tongue again.

And thank god he does. I needed to get out of my head like never before, and he knows exactly what I need. He's taking me away from my problems, if only momentarily, and I am so, so grateful.

I shiver in the night breeze, the surface of my wet skin turning into goosebumps. But I don't want him to stop. I need to feel good. Desperately.

I drop my head back and my body convulses in orgasm. It's sweet and delicious and I am floating in ecstasy. After a minute, Bogdan positions his hips between my legs. He rests his cock at my opening and takes hold of my waist.

"Guide me, baby. Guide me inside you," he says quietly.

I take his heavy cock and hold it while he enters me. He slides through my fingers into my pussy until he's fully seated. I groan from the fullness and rock my hips in time to his pumping.

"This is going to be fast, baby. I'm tired as fuck. But I can't go to bed without making you come at least one more time."

I laugh and realize I am happy. I don't know why, nor do I know how long it will last, but I can't worry about that now. I want to hang onto this feeling as long as I can, or at least for as long at Bogdan fucks me. I dig my fingers into his biceps for purchase and brace myself before I come again, just in time, because seconds later my release arrives, rushing through and over me like a big wave. Instead of pulling me under, like everything going on around me, I'm riding it, high, all the way to shore.

"Jesus, I need some sleep," Bogdan says, catching his breath while he pulls out of me. He lifts me back into the pool, and we swim across it to the steps. There is a pile of towels on a table, something Karol always made sure were available, and we each help ourselves to one. I think we each wonder who will do that now, make sure clean towels are available at the pool.

But neither of us says anything, at least not about Karol.

"Want to spend the night in my room, pretty girl?" Bogdan asks, pulling me to him once we're wrapped in towels.

I think for a moment. "You know, I think I'll hang out here for a while. See if I can stay awake until the sun comes up."

"Ah. Well, darling, you will have to tell me how it is, because if I wait a moment longer, I will fall on my face."

"I'll think about it," I laugh, and kiss him, I'm not sure whether goodnight or good morning.

———

CHAPTER EIGHTEEN

FEDOR

"Nanette, good morning to you."

On the terrace, I take a seat across from Abby's mother, who looks up at me and smiles. The resemblance is striking and I wonder if this is an indication of what Abby will look like when she's older.

If so, I will be a very happy man. That is, assuming Abby's still part of my life. Which is a ridiculous thing to be thinking about.

And yet.

I've not yet had any alone time with Nanette and am eager to know her better. I want her to know me better, as well.

There's a messy pile of clothing on the other side of the pool. I imagine a couple people must have had a very nice time last night...

"Fedor, good morning," she says. "Can I pour you a coffee?"

This woman is beautiful and elegant. How the fuck did she ever end up with Madden? And how is it he was stupid enough to let her get away?

The man defies all logic. Wants to kill his daughter for her money? Won't collaborate with one of the strongest organized crime factions in the world? Lets a woman like this go?

I just don't get it.

But it's not my problem. I take my coffee and sit back, enjoying our incredible view. With Karol gone, we are on our own for a number of things, not least of which is morning coffee unless Chef feels like making it. But it seems like Nanette has that covered. Bless her.

She leans slightly toward me over the table. "Fedor, I want to thank you for everything you've done for my daughter. I intend to thank Bogdan and Ilya too, but I'm doing it one-on-one so you know how sincerely I mean it."

I nod, a trifle embarrassed. I mean, she has no idea of the things we've done with Abby. And what Abby has done for us.

She's lucky to have such a mom. Of course, it's tragic they were separated for so many years, but they seem on their way to making up for lost time. That is, if we can keep Abby safe. And alive. That's going to take some work, although I think I know where we'll start.

By taking care of that bastard, Madden.

When I passed Bogdan and Ilya on their way out for a jog this morning, they let me know about a request Abby made.

She wants her father out of the picture, realizing it's the only way she'll ever be safe. And she's right.

While I understand it, I can't deny I'm a little surprised. That she's ready to say goodbye to a man who's been her father for twenty years is intense. But her will to live is clearly stronger.

"Nanette, it is a privilege to look after Abby. In fact, to celebrate her birthday, we got her a chocolate cake. She told us that's her favorite."

Her eyes fill with tears. "How sad is it that I don't even know that little detail about my daughter, that she loves chocolate cake?" She places a shaking hand over her mouth and her eyes well with tears. "But you know, Fedor, I have so much to be thankful for. Today is my little girl's twenty-first birthday. And to think I'm actually spending it

217

with her. I... I had lost hope this would ever happen. It's like a dream coming true. And a nightmare finally ending."

It must have been horrible, being separated all those years. And I can't imagine how Madden could have been so cruel as to orchestrate it all.

Nanette clears her throat and stands. I get the feeling she needs a moment to herself. "I think I'll go cut up some fruit I bought this morning in town. I wonder when Abby and the guys will be back. We can all eat together."

My gaze snaps in her direction. "Nanette, Abby's not with Bogdan and Ilya. I saw them on their way out to jog before I joined you. Isn't Abby still in bed?"

She frowns. "What?"

I head to Abby's bedroom. I push the door, already open a crack, and see that her bed hasn't been slept in.

Where the fuck is Abby?

Nanette's right on my heels. "What's going on? Fedor, tell me, please."

Fuck, fuck, fuck.

Before I can say a word, the front door to the villa opens and Bogdan and Ilya enter, wiping sweat from their brow and arguing loudly about some sports team.

But when the see the expression on my face, they stop short.

They instantly know.

Without needing to ask, the first thing each of us asks is whether she took off on her own. Would she do that? With her mother here?

Or is her mother part of it?

I scratch that idea. Nanette is more upset than any of us. If Abby did bolt, her mother had nothing to do with it.

Abby wouldn't leave on her own, and I seriously doubt she'd leave her mother. She knows she's safer with us than anywhere else. And she knows if she were to take off, the consequences could be very grave. Like deadly grave. She knows we guys don't put up with any shit, even if it is from her.

Even if we are wrapped around her finger.

"Where is she?" Bogdan asks, pushing past me and into her room.

Nanette speaks up from behind us. "I... I thought she was with the two of you," she says in a small voice.

"And I thought she was still in bed," I add.

"Goddammit," Ilya yells, staring at her unmade bed. "Who saw her last?"

"Me," Bogdan says, walking around her room.

"We were at the pool till late. Or should I say early? We had a swim and I came in to sleep. The sun was about to come up and I think she wanted to watch it. I should have stayed with her. But I thought she'd be safe on the terrace, on our property."

Nanette sobs as little Bonita runs into the room from the yard where she was lying in the sun. She circles the room frantically, no doubt looking for Abby. I bend to scoop her up, but she wanted none of it. So I set her back down and let her continue to search for her momma. Her panic and sad whining is the perfect representation of how the rest of us feel. She's just better at expressing it.

"Hey. Over here," Nanette calls from Abby's closet.

I peer into the large walk-in space and see that the dresser drawers have been rifled through, as if someone had dressed very quickly. There are hangers on the floor, and Abby's favorite Converse Chucks are nowhere to be seen.

She took the only thing she had in her possession when she arrived on the yacht. What does that mean? Was she going someplace familiar?

Like Miami?

Nanette picks up Abby's sketch pad, the one she was teaching herself to draw with, and turns it over to the open page it was left on. There's one word scrawled in Abby's signature red lipstick.

HELP.

Nanette crashes to her knees, and while I remain standing, it takes a lot of effort. My morning coffee turns into churning acid, and I wonder if I'm going to get sick.

Because I am pissed. Fucking over-the-top pissed.

I clench my fists, willing someone to look at me the wrong way so I can rip their head off. Hoping someone would walk through the door and say the one thing that would give me permission to drag them into the deep end of our pool and hold them down until the last bit of life is snuffed out of their lungs.

I am exploding with a rage I don't think I've ever experienced, and I'm inches from losing my shit.

First, there was Abby's dad trying to do her in. Then, when the amateur he hired failed, he convinced Karol to betray us and do the job.

And now she's gone. That fucker Madden somehow got through our defenses. That's never happened. I'm not happy about it.

And I can see the guys aren't, either.

I can't believe I doubted our girl for a moment.

That I thought she might had left of her own voli-
tion. She might want out, but she wouldn't do this
to us.

No, it was someone else. And that someone is
going to pay.

Sooner rather than later.

CHAPTER NINETEEN

ABBY

"Happy birthday, baby girl."

Funny. My father is using the same endearment the guys use for me, only in a different language. Regardless, it doesn't have the same meaning. How could it?

The man wants me dead.

I stare at him over his massive designed-to-impress desk. I'd always thought it was a work of art, the intricate carvings in the wood, the massive heaviness of it.

Today all I can think is how it's just a hollow piece of shit, a veneer that unsuccessfully shields the lame excuse of a man who sits behind it,

MIKA LANE

pulling the strings of all his little puppets, like he's some sort of god.

Oh, do I hate him right now. The streak of grey in his hair that I always teased him about only ages him now. The crinkles in the corners of his eyes, which I thought were distinguishing, are vulgar given his cold stare. And his overly-whitened, capped teeth are so fake-looking I want to ask him what the fuck his dentist had been thinking.

"My birthday was *yesterday*. Not that I'd expect you to remember that, given how intent you've been on killing me."

Yup. My birthday was spent on a private plane traveling from Spain to Miami. What a way to start the year.

His grin falters, but only for a moment. Even though he wants my money more than me, I guess he still feels some sort of fatherly attachment. But do I have any sort of familial feeling for him?

Fuck no.

"So clever," —I nearly slip and call him *Dad*— "how your minions snagged me, peacefully dozing by the pool as the sun came up."

Wearing only a towel, I might add.

"Aw, no hard feelings. At least they let your slutty ass get dressed before they brought you to the plane. Tell me, were you having sex with all

224

those Russian bastards? Was it willingly? Or did they force you?"

The smile on his face turns my stomach. Either way, I could tell the sick fuck would enjoy the answer.

"When did you become like this? I always thought you were a good man." I don't add decent father. I'm not going to be that nice. I no longer have it in me.

Clicking his tongue, he shakes his head. "My little Abby. Always so naïve. I can see my sheltering you has paid off. Or not. You have no idea how the world works. And now, I dare say, you never will."

I hope the hate in my eyes matches what he's throwing my way. It may be my only true weapon.

"How did you get me back in the country with no passport? No customs?" I ask. I'd been wondering how this would be handled the entire journey, and even more so when the private jet that had flown me landed and I was whisked into a waiting car.

How is that even possible?

"Abby, you know that with enough money, you can make anything happen. Anything. Which is why I need yours."

I wondered if he was going to bring that up. He's never been one to beat around the bush.

"I'm guessing you need it for something having to do with the Russians. But tell me, why didn't you just kill me? Why drag me all the way back here? So I can die in front of your eyes? In the home I grew up in? Is that what you want?"

I'm getting pissed now and am nearly leaning over his desk. "Is that what will make you happy? Satisfied with your life?"

He leans back in his chair, the poster child for smugness.

But this is nothing new. He's always been like this. I guess I'd ignored it. Chalked it up to 'oh, that's just Dad.'

And now that my eyes are finally open, all I see before me is ugliness. Hate. Arrogance. Entitlement.

And loneliness. How alone this man must be.

"I figure it's the least I can do to face you one more time. After all, it's what I did with Nanette, your mother," he scoffs like her name is a dirty word.

"But you didn't kill her. You just sent her away."

He scoffs. "Sounds like you've been in touch with her, my ex-wife and mother of my daughter."

"I have, as a matter of fact. The guys found her."
I tip my chin up defiantly.

Unbothered, he waves his hand dismissively.
"No matter. All that's important is that the stupid
woman put the money in a trust for you, and hired
someone idiotic enough to let me know about it. I
wasn't going to do anything about it. I didn't care
if you got her money or not. Until I realized I
needed it. So, lucky me that some administrative
mistake revealed your mother's intentions. Not to
mention whereabouts."

"Yeah, well, don't get any ideas. She's with the
guys on the island."

He laughs. Again. "Yeah, right. She's about as
safe there as you were. I could have her here
tomorrow if I wanted. But I don't. That woman
can rot in hell for all I care."

How does a person become so hateful, and
right under my nose? All the years of raising me, I
had no idea my father was capable of anything like
this. That he was this sort of person.

It's devastating, really. I mean, how does one
recover from something as soul-destroying as this?

"So, Abby," he says, glancing at his watch, "I
have a dinner engagement and need to get going.
I'd invite you but... I can't. Before I leave, I want to
give you some options. You can give the money to

me—just sign it over—or I can kill you, in which case I'll get it anyway. Which do you want?"

Before saying anything, I slowly take the chair opposite my father's desk. I am tired. So tired. I drop my face into my hands and rub my eyes. ""You know," I say without looking at him, "if you'd told me you needed the money, I would have given it to you, no questions asked. So take it. Take it all. I don't want it. It's dirty money. I don't want anything from a low-life like you. I'm ashamed you're my father."

He stands and walks around to my side of the desk. I should be scared, but I'm not. I just don't care anymore. I've spent too much time afraid. I'm done.

He chuckles and I finally look up at him. "Now, now. No need to get nasty." Taking one of my hands like he's going to hold it, he squeezes. Hard. My bones crunch and grind.

I scream.

"Let go!" I gasp, the pain intensifying. I desperately try to pull free, but he grips tighter.

Holy hell, my father is trying to break my hand.

"Stop it," I yell, getting to my feet. I attempt to kick him but he's fast and is unfazed.

"Fine," I scream. "Break my hand. Take my money. You're going to do what you want anyway.

But just know that your grandchild will never know you. You'll never see his face. You'll never hold him or hear him laugh or cry. *Never!*"

The pressure ceases a bit. I've thrown him off course. "What? My *what?*" he demands.

Yeah, take that, you fucker.

I'm nauseous from the pain in my hand and look for something on his desk to hit him with. A letter opener or a stapler. Anything. But there's nothing within reach, as if he cleared it before I arrived.

"Yes, *Father*," I spit, "you're going to be a *grand-father*, you bastard! And you will never meet the child! *Never*," I hiss with satisfaction.

Just then, a crash at the office door distracts him. I wrest my hand away as Bogdan, Ilya, and Fedor barge in. Bogdan pulls me out of the way, and Ilya and Fedor descend on my father with their guns drawn.

I begin to shake with relief, my knees buckle, and the tears start. Bogdan supports me, pulling me to him, stroking my back, and whispering calming words in my ear.

But I have only one concern. "My mother, Bogdan. Where is my mother?"

He smiles at my worry. "She's back at the villa.

We thought it best that she not come. Besides, someone needed to watch the puppy."

I give a small laugh. Relief washes over me like a comforting blanket, which I desperately need amidst this flood of emotions hitting me from all sides.

My dad's hands are behind his back, zip-tied, and Ilya and Fedor lead him toward the door.

"Abby, before we... take care of your father, what was it you said about him becoming a *grand-father*?" Ilya asks.

Oh yes, that. I hadn't wanted them to know just yet.

But too late. I grin. I can't help it.

All three guys look at me, their eyes wide. "Are you serious?" Fedor asks.

"Yeah. Was that some sort of joke?" Bogdan adds as my dad glowers at each of them.

I wipe my tears as the ugliness of the past hour is eclipsed by the good, if unbelievable, crazy as hell, news. And resulting happiness. "It's no joke," I say, beaming. "Yes, he's going to be a grandfather."

Silence.

So I help them along. Men can be so thick-headed. "This means you guys are going to be *fathers.*"

More silence.

Guess I need to show them the damn pregnancy test, which Mom got for me when she went into town. The word *Mom* feels good in my mouth.

"Holy fucking shit," Ilya mumbles after a moment, his voice barely above a whisper.

And because of course, my father butts in to try and ruin the moment. "I *knew* you were doing these gangsters, you little whore!" he shouts.

Uh-oh.

He should have kept his big mouth shut, especially with his hands tied behind his back, because Fedor pops him in the mouth. Not hard enough to knock him out, but it does quiet him as blood seeps down his chin and onto his expensive shirt.

It's a sad sight. Pathetic, too. And after all that's happened, I find I still have compassion for him. He's a damaged man, clearly, and that's not going to change. I am sad for him. So sad.

Sad for me, too.

"Abby," Bogdan asks, still holding me upright, "what do you want us to do with your father? You decide."

I look at the man I loved and respected, all those feelings now gone, like they never even existed. It's strange. And overwhelming. My heart's breaking, but it's his life or mine. Not to mention my baby's.

Taking a deep breath, I'm about to say something no daughter ever should. "Well, I'd like an apology. And then you can take him and do with him whatever you did with Karol."

I almost choke on those last words. They are razors on my tongue, and as soon as I utter them, I am filled with shame.

But I hang onto my resolve. I have to.

At this, my father begins to fight his restraints. But he knows he's fucked. His efforts are fruitless.

"C'mon, Madden," Ilya says. "You heard your daughter. Wouldn't you like her to remember you as saying something nice with your last words?"

My father drops his head, and his sudden compliance is... disconcerting. He's accepted his fate. He's lost the battle. Hell, he's lost the whole war.

"Please. Please don't hurt me," he begs, his voice wavering.

Wow. Not such a big guy any more. Guess anyone can be humbled when their life is on the line.

Undeterred, Fedor rolls his eyes and keeps directing him toward the door. I don't know what they're going to do with him. I don't want to know.

"It's a little late to be asking for a pardon, don't

you think, Madden? You've had ample opportunities to set things right. Seems being a decent human is just not in your DNA, buddy," Ilya adds.

But my father turns to me, as if an appeal might possibly do him any good at this point. *After* he called me a whore, I might add.

"Abby. Tell them. Tell them to let me go. Think of your baby. How can you become a mother when you know you had your father killed? Please, Abby, please," he cries.

I am disgusted with him, but also a little disgusted with myself, that I can be so callous. But is it callous? My life is not the only one at stake here. My baby's is too. And everyone knows a momma bear will do anything to protect her child.

It's fucked up, to want to off your father. I mean, who does that? But I choose *me*. I choose *my life*. I choose *my child's life*. It's my father who forced me to make these choices, and while I don't want to make them, I have. Without regrets. Sorrow, yes. But no regrets.

"Goodbye, Dad."

CHAPTER TWENTY

BOGDAN

I CHECK ON ABBY, who has slept the entire return flight to Spain. A heavy curtain walls off the small bed where she conked out as soon as the plane left the ground. She's been through a ton of shit in the last few days, and it's clear the toll everything has taken on her.

Not to mention that she's with child. And while I don't know shit about these things, I remember hearing once that pregnant women need a lot of sleep, at least in the beginning.

She's *pregnant.* I keep repeating that in my head to help it sink in. I'm going to be a *dad.* As are Ilya and Fedor. An honor we will all share equally.

Mind. Blown.

"Abby," I say softly. "*Malishka*, time to wake up."

I stroke a thumb over her soft cheek and her eyes slowly open. I'm dying to kiss her—and more —but there will be time for that later.

"Wow. I fell asleep," she says groggily. "For how long? An hour or two?"

I hand her a bottle of water, which she chugs until it's empty. "Mmmm. So thirsty." She wipes a dribble off her chin with the back of her hand and looks around sleepily.

Fuck, she's gorgeous, all sleepy and bed-headed.

"Darling, you slept nearly eight hours."

She shakes her head in disbelief. "Are you kidding? I slept that long? We must be getting close to home then. I mean, Spain."

Interesting slip-up.

I help her sit up, and she stretches and yawns.

"We are. Come join the guys and me. You need to eat something." I reach for her hand and help her up. She's still groggy, so I am careful to guide her. After all, she's precious cargo—even if she weren't carrying our child.

She takes a seat in the club chairs circling a table and reaches for a small sandwich. "Oh my god, guys. I can't believe I slept the whole flight.

Hey, how did you find me at my dad's? I've been wondering since you stormed his office."

"One of the losers he paid to snatch you from the villa caved pretty easily. It's amazing what a few euros can buy. And your father's cheap, so he hadn't instilled much in the way of loyalty," Ilya says.

She lets out a big rush of air. "Wow. But you got to me so fast."

Fedor nods. "Yeah, well, it's not hard to do if you have enough money."

He's right. That's pretty much how it works. We can afford to hire private jets on a whim for this sort of thing.

But hell, even if we couldn't have afforded it, we would have found a way to make it happen. After all, our girl was in danger. There's nothing more important than keeping her safe.

She puts a hand to her chest and shakes her head sadly. "I can't believe my dad ever thought he could best you guys. I mean, what a fool. I feel for the man, that he was that out of touch. But on the other hand, he's an evil bastard," she says sadly.

I get her ambivalence. He's her father, after all. Or *was* her father. But I keep that bit of information to myself.

Which reminds me, I need to confirm with our

security people the manner of disposal they chose. Of course, I'll do that out of Abby's earshot. She doesn't need to know the gory details of her father's undoing. She's suffered enough.

"Speaking of parenthood, Abby, who's the father of the baby?" Fedor asks.

I know this has been eating at him. He could hardly wait for her to wake up to ask.

But Abby just shrugs. "How should I know? Could be any of you. We can do a paternity test if you want. But I prefer not knowing. That way, you're all equally the baby's father."

Well, damn. I hadn't even thought of that. I figured we'd identify which of us is the baby daddy, and that would be that. But Abby is right. Do we really need to know? *I* don't. I glance at Ilya and Fedor.

"Guys? You good with that?" I ask.

They nod slowly, accepting this different approach.

"Sounds great," Ilya says.

"Yup. I like it," Fedor says. "Does your mother know?"

"Yup. She's the only one. Well, she *was* the only one." Abby laughs and the airplane fills with her musical laughter.

We're all silent for a moment, and my ears pop

from the plane's slow descent. It was a good flight back, although flights are always good on a private jet. There's just no downside. The guys and I talked a lot of business, ate dinner, and played poker.

I won.

And of course, we checked on our sleeping beauty. Frequently.

"We're proud of you, Abby," Fedor says.

Her smile fades and sadness washes over her face. "For what? Sending my dad off to the firing squad? I'm not exactly mother-of-the-year material, am I?" she says with an edge of bitterness.

I reach for her hand. "Baby, you did what you had to do. It was hard. Very hard. But when it came down to it, your father left you no choice. It was you or him. That's the bottom line," I say.

She nods. "I know, Bogdan. I know. It will just take some getting used to."

"Becoming a mother is going to take some getting used to, darling. But I know you'll be a champ. And look, I'm sure your mother will be right there to help whenever you need it."

Whenever *we* need it. Fuck, I am totally unprepared to be a father. But I'll figure the shit out.

Abby's face brightens at the mention of her mother. She got rid of a bad parent but gained a good one. That's pretty fucking rich if you ask me.

MIKA LANE

Fedor reaches in his pocket and pulls out Abby's passport. He slides it across the table toward her.

"What? Where did you get this?" she says, staring.

Then, realization flashes and she chews her lower lip. "Oh. Right. You got it from the French sisters. Good of them to get it to you."

Yeah. I won't explain they were paid for their bad deeds, for bringing Abby to us. She's had too much shit happen recently to deal with another betrayal.

But I can promise one thing.

These are the last betrayals she'll face. The three of us will protect her with our lives if we have to. No one will mess with her again.

And live to talk about it, that is.

"So, you're returning this to me. What does that mean?" she asks.

I kind of hate to say the words, but it's time. "You... can go wherever you want, now. With your dad gone, you're safe. You're free."

Of course, I don't want her to leave. None of us do. But that's up to her. If she wants to split and never see us again, that is her right. We can keep her no longer. And this is the moment of truth.

Stunned, she takes the passport, turning it over

in her fingers like it's something strange and foreign. She squints, trying to read the meaning of our gesture, our granting her the freedom she's wanted for so long. It's come as a surprise to her and she doesn't know what to make of it.

Are we kicking her out?

Are we asking her to stay?

Or something in between?

"Um, well, what about you guys?" she stammers.

"What about us?" Ilya asks.

"Well, you can't live without me, especially now that you're going to be fathers," she taunts.

Truer words were never spoken.

We look at each other and burst out laughing. Yeah, she's making a joke, but it's actually pretty fucking true.

"That's funny, *malishka*, because I was thinking *you* can't live without *us*," I say.

She smiles, pushing wild hair off her face, and takes a good long look at each of us.

"You're right. That's why I'm not going anywhere. And neither are any of you."

EPILOGUE

For all the time I spent thinking about how to get away from Ibiza, when it was finally time to go, I was sad. Like tears in my eyes and lump in my throat sad. My life changed so much on that little island—some for the better, some for the worse—but all in all, I'm pretty sure I've come out ahead.

What started out as a reluctant visit with the French girls turned into one huge wild ride, one that most couldn't even fathom. People go to Ibiza for its beautiful beaches and sunshine, and to let their hair down by partaking in the glitz and glamour of the island's nightlife. If I were a different person, I might have really lived it up there and gone a little wild like those French sisters who lured me there in the first place. But that wouldn't have changed the outcome of my visit, so what difference does that make? I would still have been a target for Bogdan, Ilya, and Fedor, who thought they could use me as leverage to get my dad to do what they wanted. Little did they know, I was about as worthless to my father as my mother had once been. We were disposable to him, the two of us. And the deceit, there was just no end to it. I grew up believing I'd been abandoned by mother, and will spend the rest of my adulthood knowing I was really abandoned by my father.

It hurts when I think of it that way. So I try not to.

Although I wonder what I will tell my child someday when they ask. Maybe the truth will have to suffice.

Time to break the cycle of dishonesty, no matter how ugly reality is.

As things calmed down after our return from Miami, I was actually able to finally enjoy the island— at least to the extent a pregnant woman could. Alcohol and late nights were obviously off the table, not that I missed them. In fact, I was happy to have a solid excuse to go to bed early every night and take my afternoon naps, especially in the early weeks of my pregnancy. But that didn't keep me from swimming in the ocean in my little white bikini—that is, until I got too big to wear it. To keep in shape, I took lots of hikes with my Bonita puppy, who has taken to guarding my growing abdomen like it's her own baby in there. The only person she lets touch my belly without a yip or a growl is my mother.

Something my father will never see.

I think about him, sometimes with anger and sometimes with sadness. I can't lie. I am going to miss him. Actually, I already do. But I'm missing the father I thought I had, not the one I learned was such a vile excuse for a human being. I'm missing the idea of the man I once believed I knew—certainly not the horrible one who took my mother away from me, and then tried to take my life. I still feel sick when I think about it. All those years I blindly trusted someone who was ready to throw me out like some piece of garbage.

If that doesn't fuck with your head, I don't know

what does. It will take a long time to heal from this, if I ever do. Who knows, maybe this will become a scar I carry, never far from my thoughts like some sort of cross to bear. All I can really do is believe I did nothing wrong except end up by chance with the wrong father, and do better by my own child.

The guys haven't told me what they did with Dad. I suppose they would, if I asked, but I haven't. I am afraid to. So, I imagine him on a beach someplace where he can live out the rest of his days living a simple life, not that he deserves anything that agreeable. It's really for me, this vision, creating a more tolerable picture for me to focus on. Like maybe he's taken up fishing. Or boating. Maybe he's made friends with the locals, who are teaching him how to live without the trappings of his old life. Teaching him to be kind and look out for his neighbors. Do nice things for other people.

But who am I kidding? Dad would never go away quietly, and because of that, he's probably no longer among the living, like his failed agent, Karol. Another thing I try not to think about too much.

With his being gone, I am his sole heir. I've decided to sell his company to one of his competitors—of course, someone the guys like working with. And I put the house and all its contents up for an estate sale. I don't want anything to do with either of those things. Get rid of it all. Even all my old stuff. Someone else can have it. Hopefully someone deserving.

I could have taken over the business—with help from the guys—but it's time to start over. Leave the old shit behind. Like Miami. I may have grown up there, but I never really fit in, anyway.

So, I am moving to Paris, where my mother has made her home for fifteen-plus years. When the baby comes, she will mind him or her—I don't want to know the sex yet—while I study French and eventually finish my university degree. I understand college classes in France are tougher than in the U.S. I'm nervous, but I'll figure it out. After I learn French, that is. But Mom, having been there for so long, is fluent and has lots of friends. This will make things so much easier for me.

She and I are still getting to know each other. She told me how hard it was, on my birthday, to learn that I love chocolate cake, and how heartbreaking it was to realize she barely knew anything about me.

I feel the same way about her and have learned she loves espresso, unlike me, and won't touch grilled octopus with a ten-foot pole, unlike me. The good news is we have more in common than we have differences. We're both book worms, love art, and sleep late whenever possible.

Also, we hate shopping and if we could live every day in jeans and sneakers, that would suit us just fine.

I'm not sure I see her as a 'mom,' at least not yet. I want to, but it's not the kind of thing you turn on like a switch. Right now, she's more of a big sister, which is actually pretty awesome. She's like a really good friend with whom you have no family baggage. No history of bullshit. We can create our reality any way we want. Each day is a new one. And each is better than the last.

She's going to help with the baby when it comes and she couldn't be happier about it. She gained a daughter and a grandchild all at once, which is giving her the chance to be the mom she didn't get to be with me. Second chances all around.

And then there are the guys.

Mom adores them, and they her. My life in an unconventional one, but none of us is phased by it. In fact, our new little family is what we all were craving, what was sorely missing in each of our lives, and just never knew it

While the guys have to do a lot travel with their various 'businesses,' they're calling Paris their home, now. They bought a huge apartment in my mother's building, big enough for all of us and the baby. My child will grow up surrounded by so much love, it brings tears to my eyes.

And guess what? We can fly down to Ibiza anytime we want. In fact, we'll head there for one last trip just before the baby comes to get a little rest and relaxation away from the buzz of the big city.

And then it's baby time!

When I'm heading to my French classes, walking around the city, I sometimes think I see the French sisters. It never turns out to be them. But it might some-day. Hopefully not too soon, because I don't know what the hell I'd say to them.

I mean, they did fuck me over, but look how things turned out. I could tell them to go to hell just as easily as I could thank them. Maybe rub my good fortune in their faces. But what are the chances?

One of the most surprising things about being preg-nant is how damn horny I am. Seriously. Like when evening comes, I could swear I have on occasion seen the guys retreating from me so they can get a little break. That's not going to happen, of course, because they're always available to take care of my carnal needs. But it's safe to say I am wearing them the hell out. Thank god there are three of them and only one of me.

It's intense, this new life of mine, full of love and luxury, and that helps take the sting out of the down-sides. The losses. But everyone experiences loss in their life, and if the universe is kind that day, they might come out ahead. I know how lucky I am to have my mom, my soon-to-be baby, and especially my three guys, whose names are on my lips every night when I go to bed, and every morning when I wake up.

Just like mine is on theirs.

Did you like Abby's story?
Ready to step into the next Dark Reign story?
The Devil's Captive by Mae Harden is up next.

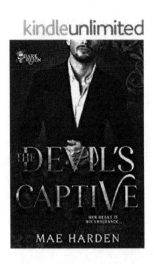

Get Devil's Captive here!

and... find all Mika Lane books here

WRONG DEVIL

DARK REIGN SERIES

Power comes at a cost and these men have sacrificed their souls. They know violence, death, and how to walk in the gray, but that doesn't mean they are without weakness. The women they love are their light and they would scorch the Earth to protect them.

💜 Check out the series and order your copies today! 💜

Their Dark Reign by Penelope Wylde
Blossom in Shadows by Ember Davis
Empire of Carnage by Bianca Cole
Ruthless Kingpin by Carina Blake

ABOUT THE AUTHOR

I'm USA TODAY bestselling contemporary romance author Mika Lane, and am all about bringing you sexy, sassy stories with imperfect heroines and the bad-a*s dudes they bring to their knees. And I have a special love for romance with multiple guys because why should we have to settle for just one hunky man?

Please join my Insider Group and be the first to hear about giveaways, sales, pre-orders, ARCs, and most importantly, a free sexy short story: http://mikalane.com/join-mailing-list/.

Writing has been a passion of mine since, well, forever (my first book was *The Day I Ate the Milky-way*, a true fourth-grade masterpiece). These days, steamy romance, both dark and funny, gives purpose to my days and nights as I create worlds and characters who defy the imagination. I live in magical Northern California with my own hand-some alpha dude, sometimes known as Mr. Mika Lane, and two devilish cats named Chuck and Murray. These three males also defy my imagina-tion from time to time.

A lover of shiny things, I've been known to try new recipes on unsuspecting friends, find hiding places so I can read undisturbed, and spend my last dollar on a plane ticket somewhere.

I'll always promise you a hot, sexy romp with kick-ass but imperfect heroines, and some version of a modern-day happily ever after.

I LOVE to hear from readers when I'm not dreaming up naughty tales to share. Join my Insider Group so we can get to know each other better http://mikalane.com/join-mailing-list, or contact me here: https://mikalane.com/contact.

Printed in Great Britain
by Amazon

24124848R00143